Madame Tussaud's Apprentice

Madame Tussaud's Apprentice

Kathleen Benner Duble

Merit Press

F+W Media, Inc.

Published by
Merit Press
an imprint of F+W Media, Inc.
10151 Carver Road, Suite 200
Blue Ash, OH 45242. U.S.A.
www.meritpressbooks.com

ISBN 10: 1-4405-8116-9
ISBN 13: 978-1-4405-8116-8
eISBN 10: 1-4405-8117-7
eISBN 13: 978-1-4405-8117-5

Printed in the United States of America.

10 9 8 7 6 5 4 3 2 1

Library of Congress Cataloging-in-Publication Data
Duble, Kathleen Benner.
   Madame Tussaud's apprentice / Kathleen Benner Duble.
      pages cm
   Summary: In 1789 Paris, Celie Rousseau lives on the streets stealing to survive, but
when she is arrested she is given the remarkable opportunity to become an apprentice to
Madame Tussaud. As the Revolution begins, she must choose between her royal patrons and
Algernon, the freedom fighter she loves.
   ISBN 978-1-4405-8116-8 (hc) -- ISBN 1-4405-8116-9 (hc) -- ISBN 978-1-4405-
8117-5 (ebook) -- ISBN 1-4405-8117-7 (ebook)
   [1. Apprentices--Fiction. 2. Wax modeling--Fiction. 3. Tussaud, Marie,
1761–1850--Fiction. 4. Love--Fiction. 5. Orphans--Fiction. 6. Paris (France)--History--
1789–1799--Fiction. 7. France--History--Revolution, 1789–1799--Fiction.] I. Title.
   PZ7.D84955Mad 2014
   [Fic]--dc23

                                    2014013250

Cover design by Erin Dawson.
Cover images © 123RF/Nadiya Struk, feverpitched, Krzysztof Grzymajło, andreykuzmin,
0mela, Milan Trajkovic, Apichart Surachartmathin, setory.

This book is available at quantity discounts for bulk purchases.
For information, please call 1-800-289-0963.

Dedication

For Liza Drury Duble: Your courage under fire and your resiliency under pressure are awe-inspiring. You are one tough girl and Boston Strong. I love you—always and forever.

Acknowledgments

As a young girl, I was fascinated with two people: Scarlett O'Hara and Marie Antoinette. I haven't yet figured out how to spend a year with Scarlett, but this book was my attempt to live for a while in the shadows of Marie Antoinette.

The idea of using an apprentice to Madame Tussaud as a vehicle to showcase the French Revolution first took shape on a trip I made with my family to London. On visiting Madame Tussaud's famous wax museum and hearing about her extraordinary life, slowly the story began to take hold.

As with any stories that eventually become books, the process is never a solo one. I want to thank my agent, Bill Contardi, for his perseverance in seeing Celie's story triumph and make the printed page.

For Marcia Strykowski and Anne Broyles, a debt of gratitude for your sharpened pens and eagle eyes that helped revolutionize my many drafts.

To Jackie Mitchard and Meredith O'Hayre—thank you for your guidance and guillotine-like cutting, shaping, and chopping. Your input strengthened Celie and Algernon and their quest for equality.

And finally, to my own little family: Tobey, Chris, and Liza, whose love lifts me up every day, who give me strength when I think I have nothing left to give, and who make me grateful each and every hour that they were put on this earth for me to love.

Chapter One

"*Mon Dieu*, I will kill you, you ruffians!"

A man's voice booms from below, and my heart leaps to my throat. The homeowner has come back, and we are about to be discovered robbing him.

I hold a diamond brooch in my hand. Quickly, I look over at Algernon. He pauses, two pearl earbobs in his palm. What are we to do? There is only one set of stairs out of here, and already I can hear the homeowner's feet pounding up our one means of escape.

Quickly, we stuff the jewelry into our pockets. In the next instant, Algernon is at the window, throwing open the sash and pushing back the shutters. He grabs my hand and hauls me toward the window. Without questioning him, I throw one leg over the sill. Then I pause. We are only one story up, but even from this height, the drop looks menacing. Fear makes itself a knot in my stomach. I don't want to do this. Before I can change my mind, Algernon pushes me over.

I tumble out, and then halt abruptly in my descent as his hand grips mine. I look up into his green eyes, and he gives me a wicked grin. Then he lets go, and I fall onto the cobblestones below.

I stand and shake myself, feel in my pockets. The jeweled pin is safe.

A shot rings out, and my eyes fly frantically to the window above. With relief I see Algernon's curly head appear, and in less than a moment, he, too, is over the edge, his strong hands grasping at the windowsill. He lowers himself down as far as possible. Then he lets go, and I catch him as best I can.

I help him to his feet and quickly push him up against the side of the house just as the homeowner's face and his musket make an appearance in the window above us.

"I am going to get the *sergents du guet*," the man shouts.

The homeowner cannot see us now, as we are pressed against his house, and so he is unable to shoot. It is a dark, rainy night, and there is no one about, or we would have to worry about strangers accosting us and holding us until the owner could come back down the stairs. But luckily the street is empty, so we can wait until he moves from the window, and then run.

It will be a race now, to see if we can escape. My blood pounds in my ears with anticipation.

Algernon and I stand pressed close together against the house, my body touching the length of his. In spite of the cold and the rain soaking us, warmth radiates from him like the sun.

At last, the owner pulls his head back inside so he can fetch the police, and Algernon and I are off. As fast as we can, we scramble down alley after alley, but it is not long before we hear the whistle of the *sergents du guet*. They are in pursuit, and I almost laugh with the thrill of the chase. I love these moments of danger, when Algernon and I stand on the edge of capture.

Down streets and alleys we dash, the footsteps of the law heavy behind us. Soon my lungs burn, and I don't know how much longer I can go on. Then Algernon grabs me about the waist and whips me into a neighborhood tavern. The barkeep gives us a look, raises a tablecloth, and we slide under the table. The barkeep drops the cloth back into place.

With my knees pulled to my chest in the darkness under the table, I cannot still the beating of my heart. It gallops with furious pulses, and I fight to control my breathing, for fear it will give us away.

Algernon must be feeling the same rush, for he takes my hand and silently holds it to his chest. Beneath his linen shirt, I can feel his heart racing, and the solid roundness of the pearl bobs we have lifted.

Algernon grins. He is so close, I can see the fine hairs on his upper lip.

"Where are they?"

An authoritative voice rings out in the tavern.

I hold my breath.

"*Pardon, monsieur?*" the barkeep says in an unhurried voice. "What are you saying?"

I have to stifle a giggle. Algernon's eyes meet mine, and I can see my merriment reflected there, for the barkeep is a friend, a patriot in our cause, and will never betray us.

"I asked you if anyone has come in here just now," the *sergent* demands. "I am in pursuit of two young robbers."

"*Non, monsieur,*" the barkeep says. "As you can see, there is no one. I am just about to close for the night. My patrons have all left."

"And no one has come in here in the last few minutes?" the *sergent* demands.

"*Non, monsieur.* Did you not just ask me this?" the barkeep says.

"You lot are all alike," the *sergent* mutters, and I can almost picture his annoyance, "protecting each other, lying for each other. But stealing is stealing, *mon ami*. And if I find you have been harboring these criminals, you will hang for it."

With that, we hear his footsteps and the sound of the door closing behind him. Still, Algernon and I do not move. We will have to stay here a bit longer to ensure the *sergent* leaving is not a ploy, for we know all the tricks of their trade.

In the silence that follows, I hear the sound of glasses clinking together as the barkeep does the dishes. Now that the danger is almost past, I am exhausted and relieved that we have escaped. I lean my head on Algernon's shoulder, and he rests his head gently on mine. He smells like fresh air, and I breathe him in, trying to ignore the smell of stale ale that surrounds us.

Then, I hear the door creak open again.

"Did you forget something, *monsieur?*" the barkeep asks, his voice bland, as innocent as a babe.

The door slams shut in anger, and once more, Algernon and I have to stifle a laugh. It will be a long night as we wait for the *sergent* to give up.

ↂ

I feel a slight tickle on my nose. I sigh and turn over, lost in a dream of brie cheese, bread, and thick slabs of pâté. The tickle comes again, bringing me fully awake to the coughs and snorts of the other criminals in our alley—and to two big brown eyes and a slobbering tongue.

A small mongrel puppy stares at me. I start with surprise, and Algernon laughs.

He is holding the puppy's tail, which he has been brushing against my cheek. Algernon has let his soft heart get the best of him again, and has rescued yet another starving thing.

"Isn't he adorable?" he asks me, smiling.

He lifts the puppy onto his lap, and the animal licks his face. Lucky dog, I think.

Algernon's hair is matted from sleep, but it cannot hide the boyish mischief of his eyes.

"*Oui,*" I agree, grumbling as I shift to avoid a rock that is digging into my side. "He is adorable. But now, we will go hungry feeding this beast, as we did the last one."

Algernon frowns when I mention the other puppy he rescued. That animal was run over by a carriage not two days after we found him. The people inside the carriage hadn't even bothered to stop. The dog had been a bump in the road, nothing more. They had driven off, laughing. The coachman hadn't even looked back.

The thought of the poor animal's demise and the callousness of the people who ran him over tires me even more than the lateness of last night.

I pull my threadbare blanket up over my head. "Let me sleep just a little more, Algernon."

"There's no rest for criminals," Algernon reminds me. "The day's a-wasting, and since the jewels we took last night will be too hard to fence for awhile, we have to work today or go hungry. So we'd best get moving."

He reaches out and pulls back my cover, and then draws back abruptly when he sees that I only have on a chemise. I quickly gather the blanket back up around my neck.

"It was warm last night," I say, in explanation of why I wear so little.

He nods, and his eyes slide away.

I sigh. I want so badly for us to be together, and I think Algernon wishes it too. But I know there is little hope of it, and this knowledge frustrates me unmercifully.

I am homeless and in this alley struggling to survive because I have lost my entire family. The Comte d'Artois's men shot my *papa* when he accidentally chased a rabbit onto the Comte's private grounds. Six months later when Maman and my little brother, Jacques, died from starvation, I had to take to the roads, unable to stay in our cottage, as I could not work the Comte's fields and pay his taxes alone.

But Algernon is here because of Julia—the girl he had known from childhood, the girl he had loved. She was killed by the guards of His Majesty, Louis XVI. They beat her to death one day when they discovered them both stealing firewood for their families. They forced Algernon to stand and watch as they pummeled the very life out of her. The guards had held him tightly so that he could not save her. When they were done, they had simply walked away, leaving Algernon to carry her body home.

After, he came to Paris, determined to take revenge against the rulers of France and their guards. He speaks little of Julia, but I can tell, he thinks of her often. He is wed to her memory as surely as if they were truly wed in life. Julia is the ghost who floats forever between us, creating a barrier I cannot cross.

"That was some fun last night, wasn't it?" he says. I know he is trying to lighten the mood between us. "Too bad we missed some things. Do you remember the house well enough to draw it, so we can try again?"

I scowl. How can he even ask me that? I have been with him for over a year now. He knows me better.

Algernon grins at my look of displeasure. "Of course you can."

He hands me a stick, and immediately familiar desire prickles my fingers. I have never been able to resist the temptation to sketch what I have seen.

"So draw," he commands me.

I begin scratching in the dirt, the stick rough under my fingers. I draw a map of the rooms and hallways of the mansion we were in last night.

When I have finished, I look up to find a look of satisfaction on Algernon's face. "You're a wonder, Celie."

I have a sudden memory of Maman looking at a drawing of mine and calling it a wonder, too. I remember her telling me my drawing abilities were a gift from God. I don't know if what she said is true. In this world of have and have-nots, I sometimes wonder if there even is a God.

Either way, what I do know to be true is that drawing has always come naturally to me. I remember everything around me with just one glance. I can tell you how many wrinkles there are around the eyes of the flower seller down the street, or the exact color of the tail on the horse the marquis rode this morning, or how many baguettes of bread the baker had in his shop window five days ago at two o'clock in the afternoon.

Some people find my abilities spooky and witch-like. But Algernon loves me for them, and his praise always makes my bad moods evaporate, as it does today.

"We'll hit them another time," he says, leaning back against the stone wall of the seedy tavern in our alley. "You'll pick their lock easily again. You always do." He smiles. "Those fingers of yours can draw the details of any house or pick the most complicated lock better than any thief I've ever worked with."

His praise swells my heart.

"But today, we will hit the *Palais*, no picking of locks, *ça va?*" he asks.

The Palais is the latest of our schemes, and a very successful one at that. At the gaming tables in the Palais-Royal, we find unsuspecting card players, and we relieve them of their cash.

Here is our ploy: Algernon goes to the square dressed as a gentleman in laces and jacket and shoes with fake silver buckles—clothes I stole for him on my first successful heist. He takes a seat at the gaming tables, waiting until a willing partner sits down to play him. Behind his opponent, I sit dressed as a blind beggar girl, tapping my cane and calling for alms. But in reality, I am not tapping for money at all. Instead, I am tapping out a code Algernon and I have devised, letting Algernon know the cards his victim has in his hand.

The idea was conceived by Algernon and is *très intelligent*. Already we have fed ourselves for days, without anyone suspecting.

"We should get going, then," he says.

"I have to dress," I remind him.

He reddens with my words. "Of course."

When he turns, I hurry to throw on a dirty skirt and shirt.

In the alley around us, other ruffians are waking with the rising of the sun, some stirring up the ashes of fires gone out, some foraging through goods stolen last night. The smell of stale urine and unwashed bodies is overpowering.

There is a scuffle down the street, where two men are arguing over the *livres* they pickpocketed last evening. The men drunkenly stab at each other with their knives. I cringe at the scene.

I will never get used to the violence that often erupts here. After Papa's death, any kind of physical altercation makes my knees weak. I still remember the bullet hole in my father's forehead and the white coldness of his skin when I reached out my hand to touch him. My poor Papa was a man who never hurt anyone, who was gentle and kind and soft-spoken, and who taught my brother, Jacques, and me to always use our minds and not our fists—but he was killed by a gun. The irony of this makes my blood churn.

I turn my head. I cannot watch this fight in the alley. If there is blood, I will vomit.

"I'll not let anyone touch you," Algernon says to me over his shoulder. As usual, he has read my mind. "I'll expose you to the pox first."

I give a small laugh. I appreciate his gallant defense of me, but I certainly do not want to contract smallpox, with its heavy fevers and ability to mar the face and body with thick, round scars. Sometimes, when robbing houses, I catch a glimpse of myself in a mirror, and I know that my skin is smooth and fair. I may be poor. There is nothing I can do about that. But I refuse to be ugly just to ward off the men in the streets of Paris.

Algernon turns back around, a look of surprise on his face at my merriment, for usually I am voiceless when violence is involved.

He puts his hand under my chin, lifting my face until I am looking straight into his grass-green eyes. His fingers are warm on my skin.

"Best day of my life when I found you, Celie Rousseau," he whispers. "I promise to always keep you safe."

Our faces are so close that our breath mingles in the warm spring air. His eyes are soft. My heart thuds hard at his words of fidelity. Could today be the day he forgets Julia?

"I would have died if it weren't for you," I tell him.

I think of the first time I saw his handsome face, as I lay dying in a ditch beside the road to Paris. I remember how gently he lifted me up and gave me something to eat, and nursed me back to health.

He pauses, as if to say something more. Then his eyes glaze with memory.

"And I'd have lost a very good artist and a master lockpick to boot," he finally says, his voice rough. He drops my chin and turns, gathering up what we will need for our work today.

Disappointment washes over me. And as quickly as it comes, I squelch it.

Why should I expect this morning to be different? And truthfully, what could we actually expect to share?

The reality is that a relationship in this alley would be less than romantic. I have seen couples here, quarrelling over a scrap of meat, no roof or bed to warm them. Do I really want my relationship with Algernon to become like that?

So while my heart might beat a tad too quickly when his handsome face is near mine, or my skin may ripple with pleasure when his fingers graze my arm, there is no room in a criminal's life for love. There is only room for one thing here: survival.

I grab a cane and don a pair of dark green spectacles. "Let's go. I'm ready to rob the wealthy of Paris."

Algernon laughs as he stands, his white teeth gleaming against the dark tone of his skin. "You are always ready to rob the wealthy," he reminds me, "as am I."

I hear the bitterness in his voice and know he is thinking of her and of how much he wishes to change the plight of the poor in this country. And I am reminded of the way the Comte's men turned me out of my home and sent me on my way, a young girl all alone. Bitterness binds my resolve with his.

I am ready. I am ready to steal from those who stole from me.

I follow him as he walks out of the alley, and into the light of the day, the puppy in his arms. A few streets later, as per our routine, he leaves my side to make his own way to the Palais, and I take the shorter route, hobbling and banging my cane about as if I truly am blind.

When I enter the Palais, I find my usual spot, sit down, and put my dirty cap in front of me for coins. Early spring sunshine has encouraged the people of Paris to meander out of doors on this fine day. The smell of coffee fills the air. I watch the people strolling about, the women's wide skirts dusting the cobblestone courtyard, the men's hats doffed to one another as they move from shop to shop, talking, laughing, seeing and being seen. Tonight, we will most likely have full bellies.

Several minutes later, I see Algernon making his way to the gaming tables in front of me. He wends his way past a harness maker and an engraver. Finally, he arrives and takes a seat, his boyish face lit by the morning sun, and pulls the puppy up into his lap. I feel a flutter in my belly as I gaze at him, sitting there.

"A game, *monsieur?*"

The deep voice startles me and reminds me that we are here to work. A tall man stands in front of Algernon's table, his back to me. Algernon waves his hand to indicate that the stranger should take a seat.

The man sits, spreading out his coattails as Algernon has done. But as he does this, I catch sight of his clothes and gasp with surprise. The man wears a jacket with emerald buttons, and a waistcoat shot through with golden threads.

A servant appears at the stranger's elbow, handing him a bag heavy with coins. I pause in my tapping and stare when I see both the size of the purse and the livery of the servant.

For the man sitting with Algernon is none other than the king's brother and the man who killed my family—the Comte d'Artois!

Chapter Two

My hands begin to shake, and I can barely catch my breath. I see Algernon frown. His look of annoyance reminds me why we are here, and I swallow my shock, and start to tap and call for alms again.

My heart pounds hard in my chest with both fear and excitement as I realize that today, I might get some small revenge on the Comte—and far earlier than I had expected.

The Comte's men had not been the least bit sorry they shot Papa. They had understood what they were condemning us to. It had been impossible to work their fields without my father, to do the work of a strong and healthy man with just a middle-aged woman, a fifteen-year-old girl, and an eight-year-old boy.

So when at last, my mother and brother died from starvation and the Comte's men turned me out of the only home I had ever known, I had headed straight for Paris. I was determined to join the group of men and women who wanted to change the plight of the poor in this country, to stop those with less from being subjected to the whims of the wealthy. I had resolved to find that group and become one of them.

Algernon's passion to see change come about is as fiercely rooted as mine. "We must stand up against tyranny, always," he tells me daily.

Algernon's penchant for rescuing things is what brought us together, but our mutual passion for change is what cemented our relationship. Both of us have been anxious to join the rebels who speak out against the king, but they are wary of new people, keeping themselves hidden in the sewers of Paris to avoid arrest.

Slowly, Algernon and I have been working our way up their ranks, meeting others who share our beliefs, like the barkeep who hid us last night. We have been given small jobs for them, delivering a package, relaying a message. But earning their trust has taken time.

So while I have not become a full-fledged member of those who work to make the king see reason, today I may still exact a small bit of vengeance on my own sworn enemy. My throat is thick with anticipation.

I have heard the rumors that the king's brother is deep in debt, but I had never expected the Comte to come all the way to the Palais-Royal to look for a game. He must be desperate indeed, when there are so many of his own people he could gamble with. Are his friends refusing him credit now? The thought delights me.

Suddenly, the Comte turns. His eyes land on me, and it takes everything I have in me to continue my tapping and not fall over in fear. Does he realize that he is being set up? Will his man grab me and drag me off to finish the job that starvation at his hands could not accomplish?

"Stop that infernal noise, girl," he barks out at last, "or move to a different spot. You are annoying me."

I stop my tapping. What to do now? If the Comte forces me to stop or move, all will be lost. Anger rises in me. Here is a chance to cheat the man who has robbed me of my family, and once again, he will win. With his power, he can take away this small chance of mine to even the score.

Algernon comes to my rescue before I can stand up and run off with the Comte's coins, as the blood singing in my veins is urging me to do. "Ah, *monsieur*. You would not deny a blind girl her chance to earn a few *sous* for her meal, would you?"

The Comte stares at me for a few more minutes. My armpits grow damp with sweat. Does he recognize me? I don't think that is possible. He was too far above my family in station to have noticed us, but then, one never knows what the wealthy actually see or think.

"Fine," he finally snaps. "You may tap for your alms, girl, but keep the noise down."

I hide my smile and begin tapping again, softly, though, hoping that the sound will soon fade into the background and be of little notice to the king's brother. Victory is now within my grasp—our grasp.

The Comte turns back around to face Algernon. He adjusts his powdered wig, which has fallen slightly askew. "What are you waiting for? Deal the cards."

Algernon nods.

I watch as the cards hit the table with a thwapping sound. When five each have been dealt, Algernon reaches for his. The Comte does the same, slowly spreading his cards as he brings them up to look at them, unaware as he does so that I can see them, plain as day.

I tap out a sequence, our code, letting Algernon know what the Comte holds in his hand. I watch as Algernon easily wins the first round.

Reluctantly, the Comte places more coins on the table. The next hand, Algernon deliberately loses, tempting his prey to play again.

Algernon goes on to win the next three hands, and the coins begin to pile up in front of him. The Comte signals his servant to place more money on the table.

I watch the silver grow and begin to dream of the food we might eat tonight: a succulent chicken, perhaps, with roasted potatoes, thin *haricots verts* in butter, pastries filled with cream—maybe a bone for the pup. My mouth waters, and my heart is full. I will eat tonight at the Comte's expense. Nothing can please me more.

Suddenly, shouting in the square shatters my daydream.

"*Arrêter! Arrêter!*"

A *sergent du guet* is yelling and giving chase to a young boy who is running in our direction. A woman in black is following close behind, trying desperately to keep up, though her corset is forcing her to stop frequently and take deep breaths.

I catch sight of the boy they are chasing. It is Nicholas, the scoundrel! A burlap bag swings from his hands as he sprints through the crowds, pushing people aside. What is he doing here? He knows the Palais-Royal is the area that Algernon and I work. We made an agreement about it not two weeks ago, when Algernon and I had first come upon this scheme. In return, I had drawn a few houses for him to rob. So why is he here, ruining my revenge?

Algernon must hear the commotion too, for he pauses at his cards, looking up just as Nicholas reaches us. Nicholas slams into the table at which Algernon and the Comte sit, sending the king's brother to the ground and upending the table. Algernon and all our hard-won coins fly into the air. The puppy yips in fright.

Nicholas scrambles to regain his footing, stepping squarely on the Comte's hand and causing the Comte to swear loudly and grab for Nicholas's leg. Nicholas kicks out violently, wrenching away. He stands and is off once more, the burlap bag still in his hand.

The *sergent du guet* and the woman in black are upon us now. The Comte's servant is helping him to his feet.

"What in heaven's name is happening?" the Comte demands, his face mottled with anger.

The *sergent* snaps to attention when he sees who stands in front of him. "Oh, Monsieur le Comte. I am so sorry. This lady has been robbed. We were giving chase to the thief. Here, *monsieur*. Let me help you."

The *sergent* reaches down to right the table, and I am about to take off, as I should, when I see the Comte's face blanch. I look to discover what could make him grow so pale.

And I see at once.

In all the confusion, Algernon has slipped away—and with him has gone both the pup and the Comte's bags of coins.

"I've been robbed, too!" the Comte shouts.

I cannot help it. I laugh.

This is, of course, a horrible mistake.

The woman in black quickly grabs my arm, ripping the dark glasses from my face. And there I am, standing in the sunshine, held fast, revealing to everyone that I am not a blind beggar at all, but a girl with bright blue eyes: eyes that can see everything.

e/3

I am dragged from the square by my hair, the crowd jeering and laughing, my feet banging hard against the cobblestones. My mouth is dry with fear.

The Comte will see me hanged. And all because today, I have forgotten Algernon's first rule of stealing: Always run.

Like an idiot, I lingered to enjoy my revenge.

When we reach the closest prison, the *sergent* throws me into a dank cell, pushing me so hard that I fall onto the straw that reeks and crawls with lice. I hear the heavy thud of the cell door closing me in, and the sound of moans and dripping water nearby. A rat scurries across the floor.

I lie there, not moving, but thinking, frantically thinking. I have seen men and women hang, know the ugliness of it, the look of eyes popping from their sockets, the blackness of the tongue that protrudes as the body gasps for air. The neck is rarely broken as it should be when the body drops. It is not a quick way to die.

My hands shake, and I dig deep for strength.

If I am to be hanged, then I will go to my death with dignity. I will not weep like a coward. And so I force myself to sit up and scrub away the dirt on my face. I straighten my skirts and prepare my face: ready, defiant, the same strong girl who watched dry-eyed as her mother and brother were buried just a year ago.

That day, I had stood there unflinchingly as the Comte's fat and well-paid priest prayed over them. I did not cry as they were lowered into the hastily dug hole in the churchyard. And when that self-serving little toad of a holy man had held out his hand for payment, I had spit in his face.

Today, I will be strong again. I will stand here without fear and self-pity, but with obstinate courage. I will die in a fashion that would make Maman and Papa proud.

A few minutes later, I hear the key turn in the lock. I stand, and the cell door swings open. The *sergent* who arrested me is there with the lady whose bag Nicholas stole, and behind them both, my sworn enemy, the Comte d'Artois.

The Comte sniffs, putting a lace hanky to his nose. "*Mon Dieu,* it smells in here."

"Is there not a bigger space in which we may question the girl?" the lady asks, looking nervously around. She lifts her skirts an inch or so, showing sturdy boots beneath.

"Perhaps the Comte's brother, the king, will lend us one of *his* rooms, so you will be more comfortable, *mademoiselle?*" I say with what I hope is a sneer on my face.

But I pay for it.

The *sergent* reaches out and slaps me hard across the face. I wheel back into the wall.

"Enough sass, girl," he says. "Who stole this man's money and this woman's bag? Tell us at once."

He is on me, grabbing my arm, his fingers digging so deeply into my skin that I wince. My cheek aches from his blow.

But I stand my ground. "I'm no snitch!"

The Comte waves his hanky in front of his face again. "If she will not confess, then hang her."

There they are. The two little words I knew would be coming. And yet, when he speaks them, my stomach lurches. My love for living has betrayed me, and I curse myself for it.

"You waste our time, child," the lady suddenly snaps, her unease in the prison cell obvious. "There is nothing in my bag of value, anyway. The boy who stole from me will find only wax heads inside, and nothing more. Those heads will be worthless to him, but for me they represent countless hours of work. I want them back."

If my situation were not so dire, I would laugh. Nicholas has stolen some *wax heads*? What a surprise he will have when he opens that bag! But who can laugh when the state of my *own* head is at stake?

"Speak for yourself, *mademoiselle*," the Comte says, his face twisted and angry. "My bag was filled with coins—my coins, many, many of my coins."

His anger gives me strength. I press my lips firmly together.

Then the lady pulls out a piece of parchment paper and a charcoal pencil from her waistband. I stare at the drawing tools as she walks toward me. I have never seen paper so fine.

"Perhaps you could *draw* our criminals for us so that we may pass the likeness on to the *guet*, and they can find them," she says to me. "Then, with a clear conscience, you will be able to tell your friends that you did not give them away by *telling* on them. And maybe you will be given prison time rather than the rope."

I look at the paper. My fingers flutter at my side. How can this woman know the one thing in the entire world I cannot resist? How can she have guessed? Is she a seer or a witch, able to read people's lives through their faces?

"That is an excellent idea, *mademoiselle*," the Comte says.

"*Merci*, Monsieur le Comte," the lady answers.

"You know me?" the Comte asks in surprise.

"I do, *monsieur*," she answers. "I am often at Versailles, working with your sister, Madame Élisabeth. I am tutoring her in waxmaking."

"Ah, I know you now," the Comte exclaims. "You work for Monsieur Curtius. I have seen your art. It is good. You did the head of the writer Voltaire, I believe. It was quite extraordinary."

The lady nods, acknowledging the Comte's praises.

The Comte's brow wrinkles in concentration as he snaps his fingers. "But your name? I can't recall your name."

"Marie Tussaud, Monsieur le Comte," she answers.

"Ah, yes," the Comte says, smiling. "They call you Manon, n'est-ce pas?"

The lady inclines her head. "*Oui, monsieur.*"

I listen to them prattling on, my mind racing. It isn't fair that I will be hanged or imprisoned for Nicholas's crime. But I can't give him away, either. And I definitely will not betray Algernon. But there is that parchment, all shiny and clean, tempting me to draw. I have to escape.

I sidle toward the door while watching Mademoiselle Manon and the Comte in deep conversation. The *sergent* is distracted too, intent on the discussion. Now is my chance.

I run for the door, but I'm not fast enough.

The Comte steps in front of me, blocking my escape. "I think not, little urchin."

Without thinking, I fly at the Comte, dragging my nails across his neck. Blood spills onto the Comte's silk shirt and lace collar, and he howls with rage.

I stand frozen. What have I done? I meant to get revenge as Papa taught me—using my mind and my words, not my hands.

The *sergent* has recovered his senses, and he yanks me hard, back into the cell.

"Shoot her," the Comte d'Artois snarls, his fingers dabbing at his bloodied neck.

The *sergent* raises his musket.

"Stop!" Mademoiselle Manon barks, and she shocks everyone by stepping between the musket and me. "I need my things back. Shooting her will accomplish nothing."

"*Mademoiselle,*" the *sergent* protests, "she has attacked the king's brother."

"And killing her will not help," Manon snaps. "I want those heads. Do you not want your coins, Monsieur le Comte?"

The Comte hesitates. Then, he sighs. "*Oui.* I do."

He waves toward the paper. "Draw for us, you stupid girl."

I cannot think. My hands are still shaking from my uncontrolled attack a moment earlier. How can I have committed that act of violence? How can I have lost control of myself like that?

When I make no move toward the paper, the Comte turns to the *sergent.* "Beat her until she does. And I don't care what a mess you make of her, as long as her hands can hold a pencil."

I stare at him in horror. My family did not raise me with whippings. Torture will most definitely break me. So what am I to do?

The lady moves closer. "What is your name, child?"

My mind is clouded with images of fists coming toward me, of having my fingernails ripped from me or fire burned into my skin—all things I have heard are done to prisoners of the king.

"I am trying to help you, *ma petite,*" the woman says, her voice rising, "but I will not protect you for long if you do not begin to cooperate."

"Celie Rousseau," I whisper, my mind still casting up pictures of my body broken and bruised, my eyes swollen and black.

Loathing fills me as soon as I speak. A real rebel would never have answered so easily.

Mademoiselle Manon nods slowly. "Well, Celie Rousseau, do you think you could draw a picture of the man who robbed me, and the one who robbed the Comte?"

I finally look at the parchment paper in the lady's hands. I can feel it again, the itching to draw, the longing to pick up the instrument and create from it. And still, I hesitate.

"Take her below," the Comte says. "We will wait in your office until she breaks."

My defiance slips away like water from a leaky pail. Fear fills my every pore. Once again, the Comte wins. And I have only the choice to obey, or to be crushed. And then, mercifully, my mind begins to work, and I know a way that might save us all.

I lift the paper from Manon's hands, taking the charcoal pencil from her, too, and spread the paper out on the floor of the cell. I touch the parchment gently, my thoughts already moving from the dire situation I face to the pleasure of my art.

The paper is so clean. I spin the pencil in my fingers, reveling in its smoothness. It is so much nicer than a charred stick, which digs its bark into my fingers. Tentatively, I apply the pencil to the parchment. The line it leaves is clear and fine.

I begin to draw, praying that the Comte is as unobservant as I suspect he is. My fingers fly across the paper. Images crowd my head—the large brass handle on the door of the bookstore, the iron rungs on the chairs of the gaming tables, the red color of the chestnut seller's cart, the worn façade of the stone on the Palais itself. I draw and draw.

A half-hour later, I put the pencil down. There is a strange silence in the room, and I look up to see the three of them staring at my work.

I bite my lip. Please let me be right.

"It is so detailed," the Comte says. "She has every hair on the back of my hand."

I let out a silent sigh of relief. As I had hoped, the Comte is gazing at the image of himself and not of Algernon. I thank the stars above for his self-absorption.

"*C'est incroyable,*" the *sergent* agrees. "Every arcade in the Palais-Royal is drawn to perfection, too. Can it truly be accurate?"

"It is," Manon says, looking sharply at me, as she moves from the open door where she has been standing to inspect the drawing more closely.

"But how can you be sure?" the Comte asks. "How can you *know* if there are two windows in the second arcade on its third floor? Perhaps there are more?"

"There are not. You forget, *monsieur*, that my job requires that I notice details," Mademoiselle Manon says. "I see them and then must work hard to remember them. But I cannot draw or remember it as she has. Her recall is superb."

I look away from her to hide my delight. She is right. I have recalled well—the face of the homeowner from last night is now Algernon's face. And one of the men arguing in the alley this morning is now the face of Nicholas. Fools! How I wish Algernon was here to share in my triumph.

"Well, we have our information," the Comte says. "Now you may hang her."

What has he said? *Mon Dieu!* Why did I ever trust this man? I wish I had pulled out his heart with my bare hands. Now, I think bitterly, he will go back to his estate for a good meal while I mount the gallows to my death.

"Wait!" Manon commands. "I cannot let you do this."

"You have no choice, *mademoiselle*," the Comte says, frowning. "It is my decision, not yours. She is nothing but a thief. And not a very good one, at that."

"Hear me out," Manon says. "Give the girl to me."

I stare at her. What is she saying?

"Whatever for?" the Comte asks. "Are you as crazy as she is?"

"Crazy as a fox, Monsieur le Comte," Mademoiselle Manon says, smiling, "for the girl has a rare gift. Her memory and ability to draw what she has seen are unusual skills. And ones that, in my business, are invaluable."

The Comte pauses, and then chuckles low in his throat. "Ah, I see. You could use her for your museum, to draw scenes for you to display."

He purses his lips and gives the matter some thought. "All right, *mademoiselle*. But let us make a contest of this, shall we? In three months' time, if the girl is not reformed, she will be hanged, and you will owe me a thousand *livres*. Agreed?"

"*Oui*," the lady says.

I watch them bartering over me as if I were a side of beef. Do they think I cannot hear? Do they find me of so little value that they will make decisions about my life without my consent?

"I won't work for you," I say into the lull.

"You have no choice," Manon replies matter-of-factly. "You work for me, or you hang for robbery. And we will find your accomplice and hang him, too."

I suck in my breath with her words. My powerlessness washes over me in a wave of understanding. She is right. Once again, I have no options. Either I hang, or I take my chances with her.

But then, I pause. I have tricked them already today with my drawing. I can think this one through, too. I am smart. I can outwit them twice.

I hesitate, my mind spinning and thinking. And then, I have it.

I will go with the lady now, but then, I will escape. I will run to warn Algernon and Nicholas, helping them take to the countryside until the fervor over this botched robbery dies down. I *can* do this.

I nod my agreement.

The Comte lets out a loud, hearty laugh, and I grimace at the sound.

Just you wait, I think. Someday, I will have my revenge on you, and we will see who feels powerless then.

Chapter Three

They bind my feet and hands. I can barely walk, and the rope cuts hard into my ankles and wrists. I stumble my way out of the prison, the *sergent's* musket pushed roughly against my back.

My insides twist and turn as if I have eaten something unsavory, though in truth, I have had nothing to eat at all today.

I hope that Algernon is not lurking somewhere nearby, for if the Comte spots him, it could jog his memory. And then we both will see the end of a rope. And yet, I am almost certain that he will be here, waiting. Since the day he rescued me from the side of the road and certain death, he has never left me behind, even when the *sergents du guet* were hot on our heels. Why would he stop now?

Rain has begun to fall, and the road before us is quickly turning into a muddy river of garbage, full of bones picked clean, vegetable peelings, spoiled meat, and raw sewage that the people of Paris throw into their streets.

Beside me, the Comte d'Artois swears as he slips in the mud, and in spite of my anxiety, I cannot help but give a ragged laugh.

He gives me a withering look and immediately raises a hand in the air. A beggar boy comes running, lugging two large planks of wood with him. The Comte tosses a coin at the child, who catches it deftly in one hand.

"Quickly, boy," the Comte commands.

Once again, the Comte's wealth affords him privileges none of the common folk can afford. The Comte will pay for us to avoid the mud, and he will not even notice that the hungry boy before him will be slick with it before the Comte is done using him.

The boy runs eagerly forward, bowing and dragging the boards heavily toward us. For him, the coin means food for the day.

The boy lays the first of the planks down in front of Mademoiselle Manon. Lifting her skirts, the lady walks the length of the plank, and then waits patiently until the boy lays the second plank in front of her. In this way, we all proceed back toward the Palais-Royal, waiting on one plank while the boy runs behind us to gather up the plank we walked on earlier, placing it in front of the one we have just crossed. The boy does this over and over again, growing muddier and muddier as the rain continues, while the four of us are wet but unsullied. The unfairness of it burns in my chest.

"Ah, there is my driver now," the Comte d'Artois says, waving his cane toward a carriage. "May I offer you a ride home, Mademoiselle Manon?"

"*Oui*, Monsieur le Comte," Manon replies, smiling for the first time, as if leaving the prison walls has resolved the dilemma of her missing bag and miraculously restored her to good humor. "If it would not be too much trouble."

I stare at the carriage. The vehicle stands before us, looking fine, all gold and gleaming, the horses' manes perfectly groomed. People from the Palais-Royal's arcades and shops circle the carriage, eyeing it with admiration. The animals shake their heads, and their harnesses rattle with silver buckles. The taxes the Comte demanded of my family have paid for the upkeep of this coach. It doesn't seem right that I should ride in it.

Reaching the carriage, the Comte opens the door. "*Mademoiselle?*"

Manon nods her head graciously. "Come along, Celie."

What am I to do?

"Hurry, girl," the Comte commands. "I am getting wet."

The Comte's words decide me.

I sit down hard, not caring that the mud of the streets seeps into my skirts. I will not get in that carriage.

"Get up," the Comte snarls. "Your filth will ruin the silk of my seats."

Looking deliberately at the Comte, I grab some mud with my tied hands and spread it all over my bodice. The smell of human waste, rotted vegetables, and dirt envelops me. The Comte regards me with horror. Rebellion may stink to the heavens, but it *feels* sweet.

I throw myself onto my side, rolling back and forth in the mud, until it covers me completely. The crowd lets out a roar of laughter. Even the street musicians stop their playing to watch.

"Get up," the *sergent* snaps at me. "Get up, I said." He kicks me hard in the side with his boot.

I let out a cry of pain, for his boot has caught me in the ribs.

Then, from somewhere nearby, I hear the distinct sound of tapping. I hold still, listening.

Go, the tapping says. *Go. I will follow.*

Algernon is signaling me with our coded words.

I sit there, mud dripping from me, rain soaking me, wishing he had not asked this of me. It will mean swallowing my pride in front of the Comte.

"She'll not soil my carriage with that filth," the Comte says, shaking his head as I rise to my feet. "Strip her. She may ride unrobed."

The crowd roars with laughter again, and my cheeks flame in panic. In order to obey Algernon, will I be reduced to standing in the streets naked? Will Algernon see me paraded to the carriage unclothed? The thought is unbearable.

"There will be no need for that," Manon responds, coming to my rescue.

I dislike the woman, but at least she has some sense of decency in her. She takes off her shawl and wraps it around me. I walk reluctantly with her to the carriage, and she gives me her hand in spite of the mud, and helps me in.

Outside the vehicle, the Comte lets out a loud guffaw. "*Mademoiselle*, I can already hear the sound of your coins in my pocket. There is no way you will win this bet. The girl is a wild animal."

"We shall see, Monsieur le Comte," Mademoiselle Manon says, smiling slightly, and then she climbs in beside me.

The Comte d'Artois steps in after the lady. "Where to, *mademoiselle?*"

"Number twenty, Boulevard du Temple," she replies.

I have never been to that part of Paris before. My heart skips a beat as the carriage moves forward, whisking me away to an unfamiliar corner of the city. Will Algernon be able to find me? Can he follow the carriage at its swift pace?

I look out the carriage window, searching for any sign of him, and then I see him, hidden discretely, but watching nonetheless. My breath catches at the sight of his face. His eyes meet mine, and he gives me a slow wink.

The coach pulls away, and we are soon on our way to the Boulevard du Temple. I sit back and watch Paris slide by. The horses are swift, and the cushions soft. I have to admit—it is a lovely way to travel.

And yet, I am not completely distracted by the ride. For when the Comte and the lady Manon are looking the other way, I lower my tied hands to my side and wipe as much filth and mud as I can upon the red silk of the Comte's seats. It is a small act of defiance, but one that I hope will make the seats smell as bad as the filthy streets of Paris for a few weeks, at the very least.

The carriage finally comes to a halt in front of a tall building with white iron ornamentation curling about its mansard roof. The rain has stopped, and the boulevard is still muddy. Yet all up and down the street, people saunter about, laughing and talking. The theater owners are beginning to light lanterns for their evening festivities. Orange sellers, oystermen, and coffee vendors call out their wares.

My time in Paris has revolved around the Palais-Royal, its shops, theaters, and exhibits. But now before me is a new street filled with as many displays, shops, and wealthy people as the Palais-Royal has offered. I think immediately of all the coins and jewelry Algernon and I can lift from the pockets of the ladies and gentlemen roaming here when I flee.

"I thank you for the ride, Monsieur le Comte," Mademoiselle Manon says, as the door to the carriage swings open.

"And I thank you for the afternoon's entertainment," the Comte replies. "Let us hope our esteemed officers of the law will shortly catch up with those thieves and return our valuables to us."

The lady gives me a quick glance. "Yes, let us hope so."

If she thinks I will help her further in finding Algernon or Nicholas, she is sadly mistaken. I have only one thought in my mind now. Escape.

"Come, Celie," Manon says, stepping from the carriage. "We are home."

The Comte grins at me, as I, too, alight from the carriage. "You are a beastly child. And I hope for my sake, you never change."

I ignore him.

At least I know that I have muddied his precious seats.

My feet are still bound, so I cannot step down smoothly. Manon goes to lend me a hand, but I ignore her and jump instead. I stumble as I hit the ground, for my ribs still ache from the *sergent's* kick.

"Oh, dear. Let me help you up there, child."

An old woman bends over and gives me her arm.

"*Merci, Ma . . . .*" I stop.

It is Algernon looking at me, Algernon dressed in women's clothing. Wisps of his brown curls poke out in an unruly fashion from his bewigged head, and his lip twitches as he tries to contain his mirth.

"*Mademoiselle,*" I finish, working hard not to laugh, also.

Clever Algernon. He has beaten the carriage by taking the back alleyways.

"I am always helping my children up when they trip and fall," Algernon says. "My oldest, who is eleven now, fell just yesterday in the alley over there."

Algernon inclines his wigged head toward a dark passageway. I understand at once. I am to meet him tonight at eleven in the alley. I wonder why he doesn't spirit me away now? Still, if this is how he means to have it, I will do as he says.

"I hope your child was not hurt, for injuries like this can often attract unwanted parasites," I say, hoping he will get my meaning, that he will understand that he is in danger and the *guet* are still looking for him.

At this, Algernon grins. "He is a sturdy lad and escapes easily from danger."

A great weight is lifted from me. I need not worry on that score. Algernon is aware.

Mademoiselle Manon comes over. The Comte's carriage has departed with a clattering of hooves.

Before Manon can examine Algernon too closely, I move to block her view as best I can. But already Algernon is hobbling away from us, walking as an old woman would, wobbling side to side in scuffed wooden clogs and a threadbare shawl. Still, Manon's eyes linger on him longer than I would like.

Slowly, she turns back to me. Then she bends down and unties the ropes that bind my feet. When she stands, she unbinds my hands, too. "There. Now you will not trip and fall again. But do not think about running away."

She needn't fret. I have no thought of escaping now. Instead, I will wait until eleven as Algernon has instructed.

I follow Manon up the stairs to the house at 20 Boulevard du Temple. The door to the house swings open, and an elderly woman welcomes us.

"You're late," she says. "L'Oncle has been waiting for several hours."

Manon steps inside, pulling me with her. "I had a little trouble. My bag was stolen from me at the Palais-Royal. The police are still looking for the culprit."

I glance around the house. The lady Manon is well-to-do, although not fabulously wealthy. The decorative wall fixtures are porcelain, not gold. Still, there are some fine prints on the wall. My eyes flick to the lock on their door. It would not be hard for me to pick it.

"Oh dear, all that work wasted," the woman says. She looks at me. "And who is this?"

"Maman, this is Celie," Manon replies. "Please set up a bath for her and get her some decent clothes. I'll go tell l'Oncle about the situation."

A door opens further down the hall, and an elderly gentleman walks toward us, tugging at his waistcoat. "Manon, where have you been?"

"Bad news, uncle," Manon says. "I was robbed at the Palais-Royal."

"After you delivered the package, I hope?" he asks.

Manon shakes her head. "I'm afraid not. We'll have to start over."

"But we need that display quickly," the uncle says.

And then, he seems to notice me, standing there and dripping mud. "Who is this filthy thing?"

"If I am filthy, it is hardly of my doing," I snap at him. "Some of us do not have the luxury of homes in which to clean ourselves."

When I see the old man's scowl, I immediately wish I could bite back my words. I do not want him to refuse me that bath. Already, I can feel the warmth of soapy water against my skin.

"The girl has a tongue," the uncle says, "and a sharp one at that. Why did you bring her here?"

"The day was not a total failure, uncle," Manon says. "I have found a solution to the problem we've been having with the museum displays. We will no longer have to worry about people complaining about inaccuracies. Look at what the girl can do."

Manon pulls my drawing out of her pocketbook. I stare at her in surprise. She has not left it with the *sergents*?

She sees the question on my face and nods. "*Oui*, Celie. You did not draw the real man who robbed us. I knew that at once."

"If you knew," I ask, "why did you not say anything?"

"You have an ability we can use," Manon says bluntly. "I mean for you to earn this favor back, or I will return you to the *sergents du guet* tonight."

That silences me.

She unfolds my drawing and holds it out for the old man to see.

"This is quite good," the uncle says, looking at the drawing. "Did you find her sketching at the Palais-Royal?"

"*Non*," Manon answers. "She did it from memory."

"Impossible," the uncle says.

"*Not* impossible," I tell him, without thinking. "I do it all the time."

"Hmmm," the uncle says, looking once more at the drawing and then at me. His eyes narrow as if I am his prey. "If that is true, then you are right, Manon. She could prove quite valuable to us."

The uncle turns to walk back down the hall. "I'll be in the study. Bring her there when she is presentable."

With that, we are dismissed. And in spite of my irritation over being discussed as if I have no voice, I have to admit that I am looking forward to that bath.

⌘

Manon's mother wastes no time producing a vat of hot water that the cook in the kitchen has boiled. I slip gratefully into the warmth of the copper tub, which has hastily been set up behind a curtain that does not close completely.

"I'm sorry for the lack of privacy, child," Manon's mother apologizes, turning once I am fully submerged, "but from the look of things, a bath was long overdue."

I blush when I see how dark with dirt the bathwater has become. But still, I will not let her think I chose to live this way.

"When you live on the streets, staying clean is hard," I say.

"I've no doubt," Manon's mother responds matter-of-factly. Then, she turns to the cook. "Marthe, hand me the soap, please."

"Baths are a waste of good water with brats like these," Marthe says, handing over a bar that smells of lavender and then returning to her wood stove. "A beating would be better for her."

Manon's mother smiles. "Children should learn through example, Marthe. Perhaps this little kindness on our part will show her how to reach out to others."

I frown. "I am no child, and I certainly don't need a lesson in kindness."

The cook snorts at my words. "See. Like I said, a waste of time."

I ignore her as I begin to wash myself. I have seen things that would curl these women's hair: children eating rats because they were desperately hungry; men fighting and killing each other over a piece of sausage; women giving birth in a crate. These women in their fancy house and their cozy kitchen have no idea what the poor of Paris suffer, or what true kindness would entail.

I hear a sizzling sound, and the smell of frying sausages reaches my nose. Embarrassingly, my belly gurgles loudly.

"When you are finished," Manon's mother says, "you must have something to eat."

With that offer, I hungrily climb from the tub and dry myself off.

Manon's mother has a silk nightgown in her arms. She holds it out to me from around the curtain. I stare at the creamy white fabric.

The gown is beautiful, but how I am to escape in it? I cannot run through the streets of Paris in a nightgown. And yet, it is lovely. For a few hours, anyway, why can't I enjoy feeling something that soft against my skin?

And so I take the gown and slip it over my head. The beautiful nightdress floats down my body, enveloping me in white folds that fall to my feet.

For a moment, I imagine Algernon's expression if he saw me now. Would he finally notice that I am a woman and not just his willing accomplice?

"That gown was Manon's when she was your age. You are about fifteen I would guess, n'est-ce pas?" Manon's mother says, smiling at the recollection as I come out from behind the curtain.

"Sixteen," I say sharply. "Just."

It makes me angry that it is not my own *maman* standing here, growing dewy-eyed with memory. But because of people such as this, she is dust now and will never have that pleasure.

I sit, and Manon's mother puts a plate of the sausages in front of me.

"Slow down, child," she says, as I shovel in the food. "There is plenty here to eat. You are safe now. We will take good care of you. You needn't worry."

The woman's concern hits me hard. Not since the death of Maman have I had a woman be anxious about me. Algernon has coddled me, taught me, saved me. But a woman worrying is different. It is warmer, truer.

I shake myself. The hominess of this place is causing me to come undone. I have to remain strong, remember Algernon and my plan to escape.

At last, I finish every bit of sausage.

"Come," Manon's mother says. "I will take you to Manon and Dr. Curtius now."

I follow her out of the kitchen and down one corridor after another, making myself memorize everything, for the kitchen has an outside door that will provide an easy escape, and perhaps we will return one day for a few of the valuable items these people own.

In spite of the quickness of Manon's mother's pace, I commit it all to memory: a crack in the third board at the right turn, a stain on the sea-green wallpaper on the left, a sconce that is slightly askew.

At last, we stop, and Manon's mother knocks upon a closed door.

"*Entrez,*" commands a voice.

And I go inside, not knowing what awaits me.

I stop short.

Wax candles burn about the room, sending out a soft light that shimmers on books lining shelves. They are real books, too— not like the fake ones many merchants collect these days to make themselves seem wealthier than they are, the ones with covers only and no insides.

I don't read, but Papa knew how. Because he handled the distribution of items from the Comte to the villagers, it was necessary that he learned. I remember him reading softly to us at night from books he had borrowed, after a day in the fields. He had smelled of the earth and fresh air. He had told me he would teach me someday, but Maman had objected. She said that a girl learning to read was a waste of time.

I understood. After all, my days were spent patching threadbare clothing, cooking thin gruel over a hot fireplace, and sweeping dirt floors until my fingers bled. One does not need to know how to read to do these chores. Still, I had not been happy with the decision. I loved to draw and believed that I would have loved to read, as well.

"Do you like books, Celie?" Manon asks, following my gaze. She is sitting in a chair by the fire, wiping her hands on a cloth.

"*Oui,*" I say.

"Then perhaps you would like to take one with you when you retire for the night?" she suggests.

I am not about to tell her I would be able to do nothing but look at the words—or that books are no longer soothing, but a bitter reminder of what I have lost.

"Let's get on with this, Manon," her uncle—Dr. Curtius—says from his desk. "We have a lot of work ahead of us this night."

Manon nods, and rises from her chair. "Come. Sit, Celie."

She pulls out a chair near a table, and I see that pieces of parchment paper and sharpened charcoal pencils lie on the table. My exhaustion evaporates in a moment. It is as if I have stumbled upon old friends.

"I want you to take a few minutes to remember the kitchen where you bathed," Manon instructs me. "Then I want you to draw what you have seen."

I do not mean to be so pliable, but my mind is already working, creating a picture. I go to the chair, my fingers picking up the charcoal pencil and lovingly smoothing out a sheet of fine white paper. I close my eyes and breathe deeply, savoring the sweetness that always comes right before I begin. How easily I am already envisioning the sparks of the fire in the kitchen fireplace, the dark black of the stove, and the soot marks on the walls. I see the one window high on the left wall, which has a small crack in its third right pane, and the copper pans, one missing the end of its handle. My mind shows me the cook with her curly auburn hair, the mole on the left side of her chin. And I have a flash of Manon's mother, with blue eyes and a small waist.

So I begin to draw. I draw and draw. Time falls away. Place falls away. I draw for a very long time. At last, I finish. I sit back, spent. I feel as if I have run through every street in Paris.

"Celie?" Manon asks, rising from her chair. "Are you done?"

"*Oui*," I say, my voice cracking with weariness.

She glances at the drawing, and then goes and touches her uncle gently on the shoulder. Dr. Curtius jumps when she wakes him.

"She has finished," Manon says. "Come see."

Her uncle rises sleepily and walks over to where I sit. He looks down at the drawing, his eyes widening. With a quick motion, he snatches it up.

I start in surprise. "That's my drawing. You can't just take it."

"It was done on my paper," Dr. Curtius reminds me. "And you may have it back in a moment."

He leaves the room.

"Where is he going with my drawing?" I demand.

"He's just gone to the kitchen," Manon answers. "He won't be long."

I have only drawn twice on real paper, and I had hoped to keep this one. I wanted to hide this drawing in the tiny alcove in the alley where Algernon and I sleep, keeping it safe and dry. Then I could lie in the dark and look at it, and remember the warmth here, and the smell of the sausages cooking, and the softness of the gown I now wear, and be transported from the sounds of snoring and belching that surround Algernon and me nightly in the criminals' camp.

Then I remember. Algernon!

"What time it?" I ask.

"Ten-fifteen," Manon answers.

"I'm tired," I say. And I am, though, more importantly, I have to escape.

"I'll show you to your room soon," Manon tells me.

Not a moment later, her uncle comes back, holding the paper as if it is a valuable painting.

"Extraordinary," he says. "She has captured everything, down to the crack at the base of the back door. She will save us much time and worry. With her help, our displays will be perfect down to every detail. She must accompany you always, Manon. You are her admission, but she must do the drawing. Her recall is amazing."

He turns to face me. "You are a treasure, child, with an extraordinary ability. So, welcome. Welcome to *La Caverne des Grands Voleurs*." He hands me back my drawing.

I have no idea what he is talking about, nor do I care. It is nearing ten-thirty. That is all that matters. "I'd like to go to sleep now."

"Of course. It's late," Dr. Curtius says. "Manon, take her upstairs."

Manon inclines her head, and motions for me to follow.

℘

I catch my breath when she opens a door upstairs. Inside is a large four-poster bed, draped in green velvet. Windows stretching from the floor to the ceiling with drapes of the same green velvet fill one wall. The curtains are of a soothing mossy color, with bands of pink embroidered roses curling down and around the fabric. And there is a beautiful shining mirror.

I walk as if in a dream toward it, seeing myself for the first time in a very long while, completely from head to toe. My large blue eyes look back at me from a head covered in blond ringlets, and though I have curves, my cheeks are gaunt.

I will never resemble the lovely women Algernon and I rob of their valuables. I look like just what I am: a peasant's daughter once, and now a captured thief. How can Algernon be drawn to that?

"I hope the room is to your liking?" Manon asks.

The plump pillows and heavy coverlet on the bed do indeed seem inviting. I set my drawing upon the dresser, not giving her an answer. Now that I am away from the spell of creating art, I simply want to get out of this place, where I am nothing but a useful commodity, and return to Algernon, who cares for me.

I go to the bed and get in, sliding beneath the covers. I sink deeply into the mattress. There is no poking here of husks, only the softness of feathers. The sheets are washed and starched, and once again, I am awash in a pleasure I have not enjoyed since Maman died. The simple comfort almost chokes me with nostalgia, but I force the lump in my throat away.

"Goodnight," Manon says. "I will see you in the morning."

She closes the door, taking the candle with her, and the room is enveloped in darkness.

I turn over and lay my cheek against the soft pillows, breathing in the scent of clean linens. I cannot believe that I am lying here in a feather bed, when only twelve months ago I was dying in a ditch. Carriages and horses had passed me on their way to Paris that day, kicking up dust that settled softly on my face. No one had stopped. Why would they? I was a peasant's daughter, a nobody to them.

I remember forcing my weary eyes open to look for the last time at the gray sky and the clouds that were threatening rain. I thought of Maman and Papa and Jacques, and how I would soon be with them, having also succumbed to starvation.

Then a shadow had fallen across my face. And he was there—a boy with mud-dark hair and sea-green eyes, a dirt-streaked face and hair-stubbled cheeks. Algernon, my savior.

I close my eyes now and envision the way he looked that day, so strong and kind. I picture my arms about him, as if he were here, feel my lips on his as if he were willing. And the quilts are so warm and my dreams so desirable, that I wish I might, just this once, have a whole night to enjoy this bed.

೫

I wake with a start and sit up. How could I have fallen asleep? Have I missed meeting Algernon on time?

Quickly, I throw back the covers just as a clock somewhere below chimes eleven. I have not slept long, and yet, even if I hurry, I will be a few minutes late.

In the darkness, I reach for a candle beside the bedside. I cannot find one, and decide it is better that way. A flicker of light bouncing within the house might alert someone, especially if they are still up.

Silently, I slip from the room, taking my drawing with me. I retrace my steps back to the library, pausing outside the door. I hear no sound from within, although I remember that Manon's uncle had said they would be working all night.

Now comes the hard part, finding my way back to the kitchen. Tonight, I make my way in blackness.

It was a short walk from the library to the bedroom, up a long winding staircase. But the walk from the kitchen to the library had many twists and turns. I memorized many details of each corridor so that I could find my way back, but I had not counted on doing so in total darkness. There is no way for me to see a crack in a wall, or a painting of birds, or a nick on a floorboard.

Still, I have to try. I have to find my way to the kitchen door and my clothes, which have been washed and are hanging there to dry.

I wend my way in the direction I believe I had come from, knowing that more minutes are ticking away. The house is eerily quiet, and I shiver in my nightgown.

At last, I find the kitchen. I can smell the scent of ashes dampened for the night from behind its closed door.

I place my hand on the knob and turn, stepping into the room.

Two severed heads stare at me, their eyes wide, their mouths open in a sick kind of grimace. Blood drips from their necks.

I let out a scream, and then, everything goes black.

Chapter Four

"She's awake, Maman."

I find myself in the bed Manon had put me in earlier that evening, and Manon herself sits beside me. My mind is fuzzy. My shoulder hurts, and my jaw aches.

Manon's mother brings a cold cloth and presses it to my face. "Poor child. You gave yourself quite a fright, now, didn't you?"

Suddenly, I remember. The severed heads!

I sit up, my thoughts swimming. What kind of strange people have bloody heads hanging about?

"It's all right," Manon's mother says, reaching for me. "It's all right."

I scoot away from her, my heart pounding. I am trapped and ill-prepared to defend myself. But I will have to try.

To my surprise, Manon lets out a light-hearted laugh. "Relax, Celie. The body parts you saw aren't real. They are reproductions made of wax. The ones you ran into are of a woman and man who stole a diamond necklace from the queen. They were beheaded a few weeks ago, and I made a wax model of them."

I remember Manon's statement at the jail, that Nicholas would find nothing but wax heads in the bag he had taken from her. Has *Nicholas* been caught? "Were those the ones stolen from you?"

Manon sighs. "*Non.* I am up making a second set of those. It will be ten days before *they* will be ready again. It would be nice, though, if the boy who stole them was found and the heads recovered."

I think of the diamond brooch and pearls Algernon and I stole. I pray that Algernon is still out there and not now in prison, slated to be executed or imprisoned for robbery. I must get out of here soon. Does the lady know I was trying to escape?

"What do you want with bloody wax heads?" I ask to keep her talking and alleviate any suspicions she might have, since she seems in no hurry to leave me.

Manon smiles. "*I* don't want them. The public likes them. Have you never heard of waxwork houses?"

I have, although I had never been inside one. They cost money to gain entry, and I have no extra to spare. I know there is a museum at the Palais-Royal. I have seen the barker outside, calling for people to come and view the exhibits. Supposedly, they have figures of famous people—statesmen, royal family members, and, I now remember, notorious criminals.

"Why do you only have the heads?" I ask.

"That's all you saw," Manon says, rising. "Tomorrow I will show you where we build the bodies. We have two museums, one here at the Boulevard du Temple, which is called La Caverne des Grands Voleurs. And one in the Palais-Royal, which is called—"

I remember the name. "*Le Salon de Cire.*"

"Correct," Manon says.

"Did you make those replicas after they were dead?" I ask.

Manon laughs. "Of course not. I drew them before they were executed. Now go to sleep. I must get back to my work. The museum is known for having the most recent exhibits, and we do not wish to let our public down."

I think about how Manon had me draw earlier that evening. Suddenly, I understand her interest in my skills. Does she mean to have me draw criminals?

"Maman, do you mind sitting outside of Celie's room tonight, in case she wants anything?" Manon asks, finally rising.

I cannot have that. How will I escape? "That isn't necessary, Manon's *maman.*"

"You may call my *maman* Tante Anne-Marie," Manon tells me.

"And as for her sitting up for your sake, that is not why she will do it. She will do it for me. I wish to be sure you stay in your room and do not try running away again."

I feel my face flush. I have not fooled her.

"*Bonne nuit*, child," Tante Anne-Marie says. "I shall be in the hallway if you need me."

Both women leave, and the room is once more in darkness.

I stare out into the blackness. It is certainly past eleven. But how am I to escape, with Tante Anne-Marie right outside the door?

There is no way I will agree to draw convicted criminals for Manon and her uncle. The criminals might be my friends. And even if I didn't know them, I am certainly on their side. I support their right to steal from the wealthy.

And I refuse to be parted from Algernon.

Then, my eyes light upon the large windows of my room, and I smile.

ひ

I tie the sheets firmly to one leg of a chair, working as quietly as I can so as not to rouse Tante Anne-Marie. I wedge the chair under the sill of the window and toss the sheets down to the street below. I will not get my clothes back, but in the criminals' camp, there are always clothes from recent robberies to be bartered for.

I throw my legs over the window, pausing for a moment on the ledge and holding on to a pillowcase with my drawing inside. Can I do this without Algernon's help?

In spite of my fear, I cannot linger, or I will be caught. Tante Anne-Marie is just outside the door. And so, holding the pillowcase with my teeth and grabbing hold of the sheet, I ignore my pounding heart and let myself down, going hand over hand. My arms shake as I slide down the sheets, and my grip slips several times.

But at last, I reach the street safely. I run on light feet toward the alley Algernon had pointed out to me.

"Algernon?" I call out softly when I reach the corner.

There is no answer.

"Algernon," I call more sharply.

Nothing.

It seems there is little choice. In this silly nightgown and bare feet, I will have to make my way through the darkened streets of Paris. And I pray I will find the criminals' camp before some other criminal finds *me*.

I stumble my way down alley after alley, straining to see ahead while keeping close to the walls. I have never been on these streets before. They are dark as pitch, and as deserted as a jail cell whose door has been left open.

My bare toes squish in the mud and muck left over from the rain, sending up wafts of human waste and rotten food. Slime runs down the sides of the buildings and sticks to my lovely nightgown as I sidle my way in the dark, the pillowcase clutched tightly to my chest.

I hear a sound and stop, barely daring to breathe. But it is only a rat digging in a pile of garbage. A few streets later, I hear voices. Again, I halt. But the man and woman who slide past me are hurrying, and do not notice me hiding in the shadows.

I long for the warmth of a small fire and Algernon's laughter when I tell him the story of how I escaped. I want Algernon beside me, with his quick reaction to danger and his determination to protect me.

At last, I come upon something familiar, the pungent smell of the river. The Seine meanders its way through the city of Paris like a long snake making its way through tall grass.

I remember my first sight of the river and of Paris, when Algernon and I had entered the city. I had been enchanted with all the grand buildings and fancy people traveling in fast carriages through the streets, carrying women with powdered wigs piled so high, they had to hang their heads out the window, for they could not fit their hair inside their vehicles. The jewels about their necks had sparkled in the sunshine, dazzling my eyes.

Then, I had seen the underside of it all: The beautiful buildings are for wealthy people only. If you are not of noble birth, your entry is barred. In this regard, the city offers little change from the countryside for France's poor.

I follow the scent toward the river, picking my way along, until at last the Seine lies before me, glittering in the moonlight that has just made its appearance through the low-lying clouds. But which way should I follow it? Right or left?

Suddenly, bells sound out. Relief sweeps over me at the familiar sound coming from Notre Dame, the great cathedral of Paris. Now I know which way to turn—away from the church and back toward the Palais-Royal.

I follow the narrow pathway along the river, taking a deep breath as I scurry under the bridges that cross the water, hoping no one evil is lurking there. There are people under each bridge, but they are all deep in sleep, curled up next to each other, the smell of their bodies drifting out along with their soft snores.

At last, I come to a spot I recognize. I take the stairs up, away from the river, cross the gardens of the old palace, the *Tuileries*, and wend my way toward the Palais-Royal. When I see the Palais with its shops and arcades and empty tables and chairs, a sort of giddiness runs through me. I have made it. I am home.

At night, the Palais is eerily empty. I run past a children's museum, a millinery, a confectionary, a distillery. Finally, I scurry along a side street and find the hidden alleyway—the Den of Thieves. The lane's dark recesses are lit by small fires, beside which people lie, wrapped tightly in stolen or discarded blankets. Some sit up, scratching and yawning as they greet the new day.

I hurry to our own little spot, tucked into the corner of the stone tavern, and find Algernon sleeping. In the firelight, his lashes lie thick against the sun-browned curve of his cheek. My eyes linger on his slender fingers, clutching at the puppy, which lies sleeping beside him. I imagine reaching for him, and it is all I can do to not do this very thing.

But instead, I force myself back to practical matters.

I bend near my boy, but not too close. He is a restless sleeper with lightning-quick reflexes. I do not want to risk a stab wound.

"Algernon," I whisper.

He is awake in an instant, sitting up, a knife at the ready. The puppy barks.

"It's me," I say, scooting quickly back an inch or two.

Algernon rubs the sleep from his bright green eyes. Then he reaches out and takes my hand. "Are you all right?" His voice is filled with anxiousness.

"I'm fine," I reassure him.

"Where were you this evening? I waited hours for you," he asks. "I was worried about you."

"I had a little mishap," I say. "I stumbled onto a room full of severed heads."

Algernon's eyes grow wide, and I laugh.

"They were heads for that waxworks house at the Palais-Royal," I tell him. "You know the one by Robert André's bookshop, where that big man is always calling out and advertising the shows?"

Algernon nods. "*Oui.* I know the place."

"Well, that's where the lady who caught me works," I say. "And that bag that Nicholas stole?"

Algernon waits.

"Full of nothing but those wax heads!" I let out another hoot of laughter.

Algernon's face lights up. "Truly?"

I nod.

Algernon's eyes dance with merriment, and he laughs, too.

"Serves Nicholas right for being in our corner of the Palais."
Then he frowns. "But that doesn't explain why you didn't
escape like you were supposed to. Did they mistreat you? I'll kill
them if they did."

I hesitate. I don't want to tell Algernon this part, but he will want his
explanation, or he will take after Manon and her family on my behalf.
"I fainted at the sight of those heads," I finally confess.

Algernon scowls. "Good criminals don't faint, Celie. Only
fancy women have the luxury of that."

"I didn't mean to," I protest. "It just took me by surprise, is all."

"Nothing should surprise a good thief," Algernon reminds me.
I give him my evil eye. Does he think I don't know this?

His gaze sweeps over me now that he is fully awake, and I see
him take in the flimsy nightgown. His eyes rest on the curve of my
hip, which is outlined by the sheer fabric.

"What happened to the pants and shirt I filched for you last
week?" he finally asks, his voice tight.

"They made me take a bath," I tell him.

His eyes meet mine, not as a teacher to a child but like a boy
might look at a girl. My heart thumps, hard.

I sit down next to him. I finger the soft fabric. "The gown they
gave me is beautiful, n'est-ce pas?"

His eyes slip over the silk and satin trim. I hear his breath
quicken.

I lean in closer, putting my mouth just inches from his neck. I
can see a vein there, pulsing sharply. I have hope.

"They gave me lavender soap," I whisper. "It was nice. Do you
like it?"

Algernon says nothing. I wait.

Then abruptly, he turns his head. "Well, I hope the smell wears
off soon. We can't have you playing the blind beggar girl and
smelling fancy. So put that gown away, and find some old breeches."

Disappointment washes over me.

"Get dressed, Celie, please," he says with an edge of anger to his voice.

I do as he bids and reach into an old pile of clothes. My hands shake. I find a pair of breeches, slipping them on. Reluctantly, I take off the nightgown, and pull on an old ratty shirt. I tuck the lovely nightgown safely under my thin blanket. Now when I sleep, I will finger the soft fabric and remember that this beautiful thing made Algernon notice me, if only for a moment.

"You didn't happen to take a thing or two on your way out, eh?" Algernon asks, his voice cracking.

"I may have fainted, but I'm not stupid," I say, my voice stiff, too.

From inside the pillowcase, I pull out a small china swan and a set of silver hairbrushes I have stolen from the green bedroom.

"Now, there's my girl," Algernon says, turning around. He sets the dog down and takes the items from me, turns them over in his hand, and nods approvingly. "They'll fetch a nice price."

He smiles, the old Algernon again. "You're an uncommon thief, Celie."

His compliments don't warm me as they usually do.

"Still," he says, sighing, "we'll have to keep a low profile for a while."

He holds up the Comte's bag of coins. Those coins should make me feel better, but they don't.

"When we finish these, it's back to robbing houses," Algernon says. "Such a shame. That card deal was working well. Did you happen to take a look around the house before you hightailed it out of there?"

"I always look around me. You know that." I lay down on my blanket. I am suddenly very tired. I have only had a few hours sleep in the last two days. And I am exhausted and humiliated from my failed attempts to make Algernon see me in a romantic light.

Discouraged, I pull out the drawing I did of Manon's kitchen, unroll it, and place it near me.

"Ah," Algernon says, leaning over and peering at the drawing, "so *that* is the inside of their fine house, eh?"

His face is close to mine. I could kiss him if I wanted to. His eyes move from my drawing to my face, and his jaw twitches. He sits up and moves away once again. This time, I am prepared for the rejection. I look wearily up at the sky.

The first rays of morning sunlight suddenly flicker in the alleyway, making me squint at the brightening sky.

Algernon stands, his eyes roaming the bodies packed next to each other. "Ah, there is that rogue, Nicholas. Let's go have some fun, shall we?"

He turns and offers me a hand up. I take it, the feel of his skin warm against mine. He pulls me to my feet, makes sure I am up and steady before dropping my hand. Then he strides away, leaving the puppy and me to follow.

When Algernon reaches a lump curled in the dirt, he gives the figure a poke with his foot.

Nicholas groans and looks up, his eyes still unfocused from sleep. "What?"

"Heard your takings at the Palais-Royal were a little unusual yesterday," Algernon says, grinning down at him.

In spite of my frustration with Algernon, I laugh.

"That'll teach you to stay away from my section of the Palais," Algernon tells him. "I see you there again, I'll give you something really unusual to think about—a good beating."

"You ain't the king, last time I checked," Nicholas spits out. "If I feel like doing a little pickpocketing there, I'll do as I like."

"Anxious for more of those wax heads then, I take it?" I ask, teasing him.

Nicholas scowls up at me.

"He may not be, but I am!"

I turn. Behind us, Manon stands with a *sergent*, both disguised in dirty old rags. They look like any of the criminals in the alley, except for one thing: The *sergent* is holding a musket.

Chapter Five

We are caught, and I am a fool! Why had I thought that this woman would give up so easily, that she would be content to let matters drop? She must have followed me here.

I should have been more careful, and I want to kick myself for my stupidity.

"You'd best be on your way," Algernon says, planting his legs firmly and crossing his arms. He reaches out and moves me behind him to defend me, his fingers resting lightly on my arm. "One word from me, and these fine people will rip you limb from limb."

The *sergent* steals a glance nervously over his shoulder at the other criminals in the alley. But Manon does not quiver. Her gaze on Algernon and me is rock steady.

"I've come for the girl," Manon says, "and my heads."

"You can have the heads," Algernon tells her.

He waves carelessly toward Nicolas. "You heard the lady, Nicky. Give her the bag you stole from her yesterday."

"Why should I?" Nicholas whines.

"Because I'll give you to the *sergent* here if you don't," Algernon says. "Now hand it over."

Nicholas turns his back on us and rifles through a pile of things lying near him. In a moment more, he hands over the bag. Manon takes it from him and glances inside. She nods, seemingly satisfied.

"And now the girl," Manon says.

"You *can't* have her," Algernon says, his green eyes darkening. "She's my sister. And even fancy folks such as you aren't allowed to take our own siblings away from us."

He pauses, then adds mockingly. "Even if we are poor."

Sister? I almost cry, for—unfortunately—brotherly is the only way he has ever treated me.

"Your sister?" Manon says, ignoring Algernon's jibe about being poor. "You must have different fathers then."

Algernon doesn't flinch. "That's really none of your business, now is it? We're family, and that's just the way of things."

"It is also *just the way of things* that men who rob the brother of our good king usually find themselves swinging at the end of a rope," Manon says softly, "and then what would happen to your *sister?*"

Her words chill me.

"Lay a hand on him," I warn, stepping forward, "and I will kill you myself."

Algernon puts his arm about my waist and squeezes a warning. His fingers graze the space between my shirt and my pants. I can feel that touch all the way to the roots of my hair.

"What is it you want with Celie?" Algernon asks.

"Her skills at drawing," Manon answers without hesitation.

Algernon nods his head, as if mulling this over. "Perhaps we can work something out?"

I feel a sudden quiver of uncertainty. Is he about to treat me as something to be bartered for?

Algernon's grasp on me tightens, so I say nothing.

"How much would you like for her?" Manon asks.

Algernon laughs. "I would never *sell* Celie, *mademoiselle.*"

Giddy relief washes over me. How could I have doubted him?

Manon snorts. "Ah, a thief with morals. Then what do you propose, *monsieur?*"

"A place to sleep and eat for the both of us," Algernon says without hesitation. He glances at the *sergent.* "And a promise to drop all charges, of course."

Manon does not flinch. "Agreed. But you will work to earn your keep. And let me warn you, *monsieur*, should you choose to steal from me, it will be the noose you'll sleep with."

"Eh, that isn't fair," Nicholas whines. "I should be the one getting food and a bed. It was me that stole the bag in the first place!"

"And it was you on my turf in the second place," Algernon says, and the anger in his voice makes Nicholas flinch.

Algernon turns to me. "Grab up your things, sister. Seems as if we are *moving* this fine day to better accommodations than these streets."

"Two more things," Manon says.

She points to the animal at Algernon's feet. "No dog. In my line of work, puppies are much too boisterous to have around."

Algernon considers for a moment and then nods. He scoops up the puppy and hands him to Nicholas. "For you. Take good care of him, or you'll answer to me."

Nicholas's face lights up. He hugs the animal tightly. I can see they are a good match, though Algernon looks a bit bereft.

"And the second thing?" I ask.

"While you are packing," Manon says, "please bring along the china swan and the silver hairbrushes you took from me when you ran away."

Manon's eyes on me are steely hard. Suddenly, I wonder if Algernon has done the right thing. The lady seems clever and quick, and I pray that Algernon doesn't think he can outsmart her. In that contest, I'm not so sure we would win.

❧

I wake the next day in the late morning and stretch myself out in the clean sheets. My wish has been granted. I have had time to sleep in this bed and luxuriate with dreams of Algernon.

My boy was smart to bargain for this. Now, we will be fed and clothed and for a time not have to worry about getting caught by the *sergents du guet*. Instead, we can work on ingratiating ourselves with the rebels in Paris while living in safety.

I rise and dress, easily making my way to the kitchen in the daylight this time. When I push the door open, Tante Anne-Marie greets me with a smile, which is kind considering I betrayed her by escaping last night.

"Ah, our little sleepyhead is finally awake," she says. "Come and have some breakfast."

I think I will faint with pleasure. Cook is spooning out a heap of fresh eggs onto a plate with sliced bread, her apron splattered with grease.

I walk swiftly to the table, and grabbing a fork, I dig in fast. The last time I tasted eggs was the morning my father was shot.

"Cooking this late in the morning isn't right," Cook grumbles. "The girl should rise at a decent hour if she wants breakfast."

"Ah now, Marthe," Tante Anne-Marie says, "she was tired from all the goings-on last night."

"Goings-on? I'll say!" Cook says. "Stealing our stuff, and then Manon bringing her back. Should have turned the three of them over to the *sergents du guet*, if you ask me."

I had not thought of this before. Algernon and I are fairly trapped in this house, there for the taking should Manon become displeased with us or change her mind. We will need to arrange an escape route as soon as possible.

"Where is Algernon?" I ask.

"That's the culprit's name, is it?" Cook says, as she plunges her arms into soapy water to wash her frying pan.

"He's already out in the salon working, Celie," Tante Anne-Marie tells me. "And when you are finished, you must change and go there, too."

"The place with those heads?" I ask, and I shiver, remembering the blood that looked so real.

"In the morning light, I think you will find that the heads are far less menacing than they were in the dead of the night," Tante Anne-Marie says.

I'm not so sure of this. Still, this is the deal we have made to escape the streets. At least for the time being, I will enjoy the luxury of a roof over my head.

Tante Anne-Marie brings me a clean dress and apron. "Where Manon will be taking you, you will need to dress properly."

"And where will that be?" I ask, envisioning crime scenes or prison cells.

"Ach, so many questions," Cook says, shaking her head with its white starched cap. "Take her away, Anne-Marie. She is giving me a headache with all her questions."

Tante Anne-Marie laughs. "You must ignore my sister. She complains much but does not mean most of it."

I start in surprise. The grouchy cook is the sister of kind Tante Anne-Marie?

"Come, Celie," Tante Anne-Marie says before I can ask. "Manon is waiting."

I follow her out of the kitchen and down a small corridor to a door I do not recognize. Tante Anne-Marie turns the knob.

"Welcome to La Caverne des Grands Voleurs," she says.

"At last!" Manon's uncle says, looking up and seeing me as I step inside. "Child, I indulged you today, but you must rise earlier if you intend to eat my food and sleep in my house. Do you understand?"

"*Oui, monsieur*," I say. But I say it automatically, for my attention is caught by the comings and goings in front of me. The rooms of the waxworks museum are lined with oil lamps and mirrors. Rich tapestries hang on the walls.

Several men and women are working to finish a display. The men are lifting and moving various pieces of furniture about. Algernon is among them, and he turns, pleasure lighting his face when he sees me.

His hair shines, all clean and tousled, and his face is free of dirt. He wears new breeches and a shirt with the cuffs rolled to his elbows. The muscles in his chest are tight against his new clothes. He looks like a handsome young gentleman doing chores on his estate, one for whom high-class women would swoon when he took off his jacket. And I can almost believe he belongs right here, among the wealthy and living this fine life.

He raises a sardonic eyebrow at my dress, and I smile, for he has noticed the change in me, too. But even soap can't erase the gleam in his eyes or the devil in his smile. He is plotting something, I can tell.

"We are creating a scene of Monsieur and Madame Baston," Tante Anne-Marie says, interrupting my thoughts. "Do you know of them?"

I nod in response to Tante Anne-Marie's question. All of Paris knows of the Bastons. The husband killed his wife by stabbing her twenty times and then cutting out her heart.

I look at the *tableau* in front of me. The women in the room are tweaking the clothing of the waxwork people, adding pieces of jewelry to the neck and gown of the lifelike display. A wax woman sits upon a chair, her hand to her chest, and her eyes wide with fright. Blood drips down the front of her bodice. Above her, a wax man stands with a bloody knife, his hand poised to bring the blade down again.

I think then of seeing my own family, each of them lying dead, breath gone from their bodies. The violence of the scene reminds me of Papa's bloody forehead, and I quickly look away before I am sick.

Manon comes out from behind a screen, wiping her hands. "*Bonjour*, Celie. Are you ready to get started?"

"Please. I don't want to draw dead or murdered people." I am barely able to whisper.

"It is not just the people I will have you draw, but their living spaces and surroundings. And I do not want to hear complaints. You have a roof over your head, and food in your stomach,"

Manon says, her voice firm. "Now you must earn those things. All of us must."

"Some people don't," I snap back, my heart thudding with the thought of drawing bloody crime scenes. "Some people sit all day doing nothing, while the rest of the world waits on them. I've seen them in the Palais-Royal."

"And do you think *you* are one of these people?" Manon snorts. "*Non*, Celie, *you* have but two choices in this life you've been given, *ma petite*. You may continue to steal from the rich, as you have in the past, sleeping in a filthy, muddy alley and starving most days, hoping you are never put in jail or hanged. Or you may work to entertain them, robbing them legally as we do, and sleep in fine sheets with your belly full."

I am brought up short by her words. It has never occurred to me that there are more ways to take from the very people who have taken from me. Could this work—legitimate work—help assuage the anger that burns deep in my gut? Can I find the same satisfaction here that I get each time I steal a silver trinket from a baroness's house, or lift a pocket watch from a marquis?

"So what will it be, Celie?" Manon asks. I can see her patience is beginning to run out.

I hesitate. I do not know if I can find the courage to face these horrors, but I can try. For food and a bed and a chance to practice my art, I can try. Slowly, I nod. And with that gesture, I begin my training.

ॐ

Manon gives me a tour of the waxworks first. At La Caverne des Grands Voleurs—the Cave of the Great Thieves—the exhibits consist of gruesome scenes of murder and hangings. Here, fake blood spills on lovely rugs. Eyes pop from skulls. Black tongues hang from severed heads. A blue light casts eerie shadows over the criminals, creating a world of sinister intents. Walking around these exhibits, I begin to regret my hasty agreement to draw these scenes.

Later in the day, I accompany Manon across town to the Palais-Royal. An odd wave of homesickness washes over me as I walk among its shops and gaming tables, smell the scent of newly baked baguettes in the air. But I know it is only Algernon beside me that I miss—certainly I don't regret having food and a bed now.

At Le Salon de Cire, the lines are long. In front of the museum, a giant of a man is shouting for people to come and see the exhibits.

Manon makes her way through the crowd.

"How are our takings for the day?" she asks the giant.

"You'll be pleased," the man says, opening a box to show coins gleaming inside.

I have seen the man often, but from a distance. He is so tall that I feel like a flea standing next to him.

"Celie, this is Paul Butterbrodt. He is our barker, calling and drawing the crowds to our exhibit. His voice can be heard above all the others announcing our shows, and that is why we employ him. Just as we've engaged you for your drawing skills," Manon says.

Paul Butterbrodt laughs. "My big girth attracts them also, wouldn't you say?" His belly rolls when he laughs.

He holds out his hand, and I shake it. I like the big man.

"How much does he weigh?" I ask Manon as we slip into the Salon.

"Two hundred sixteen kilos," Manon answers. "His voice is good, but his size is why he is so right for us. Giants, dwarves, sickly thin people, and exotic natives from afar fascinate the wealthy. They want any entertainment that is unusual or strange. His size helps bring people to us."

Inside Le Salon de Cire, the exhibits are amazing, and I begin to relax. Drawing scenes like this will be a joy.

They have a *tableau* of the king and queen receiving callers. "Is this truly what they look like?" I ask. The queen's bodice shimmers with jewels and the king's waistcoat has silver threads running through it.

"*Oui*," Manon says. "The dresses we use for the queen are made for us by the queen's dressmaker herself, Rose Bertin. We want every detail to be accurate. That is why we need you, Celie. No one can compare to me when it comes to recreating these figures in wax, but your drawings are amazing in their details. My efforts are not half as good as yours."

We move further into the gallery, Manon explaining to me who I am seeing in each exhibit: Benjamin Franklin, the great statesman from all the way across the sea in America; Voltaire, the great writer, as he sits at his desk penning his next work; the brave general, Lafayette.

"It is two *sous* to enter here," Manon explains, "but twelve *sous* to be allowed to approach and stand near the figures."

I see the attraction of this place. It makes you feel as if you have actually been among these people.

"People may hear the news that is called out by the ballad singers or peruse the papers if they can read," Manon continues. "But we *show* them the news. And we must constantly be changing the exhibits, so that what they see is in keeping with the latest information being passed around the streets. Do you understand?"

I nod.

"Now come," Manon says. "You have seen what we do here. Next you must see what others are doing, so you will know the competition we face."

❧

For the next several nights, Manon takes me from show to show, returning late in the night. I see horses dancing the minuet, a tightrope-walking monkey, a girl who dances with eggs tied to her feet, a Spaniard who drinks boiling oil and walks barefoot on red-hot iron, a fortune-telling dog, a white rabbit that can do algebra, and an equestrian show with an orchestra and jets of flame that shoot out all around the horses as they perform.

I am dazzled, even as I understand that I am at these entertainments for free, that the showmen have given Manon a pass, as Manon does for them when they are training their apprentices.

An apprentice. That is what Manon has told me I am to become. I am delighted by the prospect of drawing all day, eating well, sleeping in a bed, and collecting coins from the wealthy. Could I ask for more?

And yet, I think of Paul Butterbrodt. Does he mind having people stare at him as they go in the waxworks? And what of the girl dancing with eggs on her feet, or the Spaniard who must drink hot oil night after night? Do they not feel used by the crowds of men and women dressed in fine silks and jewels, who have come simply to be entertained?

My own family was used, too—to grow food for the Comte d'Artois and the king and for the clergy. As in all things, the wealthy rule, and farmer and entertainer are both used for the services they provide. So perhaps, in the end, there is little difference between us, and Manon is right. At least robbing the wealthy in this fashion is safer and more comfortable, for both Algernon and me.

Chapter Six

The next morning, when I wander down to the kitchen, I find only Cook.

"Where is Manon?" I ask.

"Where she should be," Cook replies, "at the king's palace with his sister."

She bangs down a plate of sausage and toast. "Eat up. My sister will be along shortly to take you to Dr. Curtius."

I make a face. I do not want to spend the day with that crabby old man.

"And there will be no more of these late awakenings," Cook continues, as she turns another sausage over in the pan. "Manon is done training you. Now others will show you the rest. And you will be in bed at a decent time and up at an earlier hour. I will no longer be making breakfast at this unreasonable juncture of the day."

With these words, Cook tosses a warmed sausage onto my plate, and I have to hide a smile. "*Oui, mademoiselle.*"

"*Mademoiselle? Mademoiselle?* I'm Tante Marthe to you," Cook grumbles.

"*Oui,* Tante Marthe," I say, and grin. Tante Anne-Marie is right. Tante Marthe makes a lot of noise, but she has a big heart. I like her, but know better than to tell her that. Tante Marthe is just like Algernon. My growing fondness must be kept a secret.

Algernon—I have not seen him in a week, and I miss him. When I fall into bed after a late-night show I have attended, it is his face that fills my dreams. And I wake longing to see him. I had not known that in agreeing to this arrangement, we would be separated so much, and I wonder if being apart bothers him as much as it does me.

"Ah, Celie," Tante Anne-Marie says as she comes into the kitchen, "hurry up, child. Dr. Curtius is waiting for you."

Inside the wax house, Dr. Curtius is sitting at a long table, working with a head, but not a wax head. This one is made of clay. He is bending and shaping the clay with his fingers, brushing down the cheeks with his thumbs.

"Celie is here," Tante Anne-Marie says.

"Leave her," Dr. Curtius commands.

Dr. Curtius does not say anything, and I begin to grow restless.

Finally he turns to me, impatience at my fidgeting evident on his face. "It is time for you to learn the process of making wax figures. Come. Sit next to me. And I will explain, for you will need to see as I see in order to draw for me in the right way."

He pulls out a stool, and at last, I sit.

"A wax head," he explains, "takes between ten and fourteen days to complete. To start, we take measurements of the head. Today, you will be my subject."

He pulls out a pair of tongs and puts them around my scalp. He measures the width of my head, and the length of my face from the top of my skull to my chin, using a piece of string along with the tongs. With each measurement, he jots down numbers. Though I cannot read, I do know numbers, as Maman had taught me the value of money and how to recognize amounts when they were written, so I might barter well in the village.

Then Dr. Curtius takes a piece of clay and begins to mold it with his hands and a knife, measuring the length and width of the piece as he has measured my head. I watch as my likeness slowly begins to take form.

"This will be a rough one only," the doctor says, as his hands pinch and poke and pull on the clay. "If I was working on a real subject, this would take hours. But as you will not be involved in this part of the process, we will move along."

Finally, he holds the sculpted work next to my face. "Not a bad likeness."

"It's amazing, *monsieur*," I say, and it is. He has shaped me perfectly.

"Please call me *mon oncle*," he says. "It is how I like to be addressed by persons younger than myself in my own home. *D'accord?*"

I nod my agreement.

"So once the clay head has been made, we cover the head in plaster," l'Oncle continues. "We do this in sections. You may help me with this, if you are careful."

Taking a small brush, I dip it into the wet paste l'Oncle has by his elbow, following his lead and smearing the material on the front of the clay head.

"Be sure to make the plaster smooth," l'Oncle directs me. "You do not want a mold with bumps in it."

I do as he instructs, applying the gooey substance over the entire face of the clay model, smoothing it out as I go along. I am absorbed completely in the task, for it is much like painting and drawing, and my fingers fly over the form. I look up at him when I have finished.

"Not bad," he says.

"For your first time," he adds.

જી

When the plaster dries on the front of the head, I remove it from the clay and cover the back of the head, letting that dry, and then the sides. When they are finished, I clean each section, and then l'Oncle shows me how to bind them together.

"I will do the next part," l'Oncle says, "but watch closely."

Taking a large pot filled with hot vegetable wax, l'Oncle slowly pours the liquid into the hollow mold of the head I have created. Steam rises into the air.

"The trick is not to shake while you are pouring." L'Oncle grits his teeth as he holds tightly to the pan. "If you wobble, the face will have lines on it, lines you do not want, and there will be no fixing it."

I watch as wax pours out in one continuous stream, until it is to the top of the upturned neck.

There is a knock at the door.

"*Entrez*," l'Oncle calls out, setting the hot pan aside.

Algernon comes in, and my heart leaps to see him standing there.

"What is it you want?" l'Oncle asks.

"That delivery of horsehair is here," Algernon says.

"Hmmm," l'Oncle says, "I'll want to see the quality of it. Celie, you may go and have your supper. The wax must harden anyway."

I nod, and l'Oncle leaves the room. He cannot be gone fast enough. I am breathless to be alone with Algernon.

When l'Oncle is gone, Algernon looks me up and down, and I feel myself flush under his gaze.

"And now you are a lady, I see, all dressed up and clean," he says, mockingly.

I curtsy. "As are you, *monsieur*. Are you enjoying good food and clean linen as much as I am?"

This brings an unexpected frown to Algernon's face. "I may be clean, but I'm still what I always was, Celie—a man who believes in equality for all men, and one who will do anything to get it. I hope you have not forgotten that that is who we are, what we are striving for?"

I shake my head, startled by his outburst. Of course I have not forgotten. How can he think this of me? I know I have been busy attending nightly entertainments, but that does not mean that our plan to join the rebels has completely escaped my mind. The desire to effect change still burns brightly for me.

He turns and runs his eyes over the room. "I've been doing a little inventory taking, and there is quite a lot here for us to swipe, eh?"

To my shock, what I feel at his words is dismay. While I still mean for the rich to pay for their crimes, I realize that I do not want to steal from *these* people. The last two weeks have been marvelous, waking in a bed, eating three whole meals every day, studying a new form of art. I would feel bad taking their things. I like the aunts and uncle, and I am sure Manon could easily track us down again.

There are many wealthy to steal from in Paris. How can I convince Algernon that Manon need not be one of them?

"I don't know. They've been nice to us, Algernon," I say tentatively.

"Don't grow soft on me, Celie," he says, shaking his head as he turns back around. "And do not fool yourself. They're only kind to you because of your extraordinary recall and drawing skills. They do not care about *you*. They are wealthy, and the wealthy care only about staying wealthy."

He pauses. "But I have a plan, and one that does not involve stealing."

Relief runs through me at his words.

"I met Mirabeau yesterday," he says softly.

He pauses for effect. "Alone. By myself."

Algernon has seen the great and nobly born orator Comte Mirabeau? How did he do that? And without me? I am resentful to have been left behind, although I must remind myself that I have been kept busy by Manon.

I remember the first time Algernon took me to hear the tall, stout man speak. He spoke with a power and a force that had astounded me, addressing the need for change and the unfairness of a system where some starved while others had more than they could consume. It was as if Mirabeau was not of noble birth, as if he had gone hungry and cold, as we had.

That day, I felt as if he was speaking right to me. He became my hero, and the hero of Algernon and the crowd. The ragged group that had gathered to hear him gave a cheer that echoed all over Paris when he finished. Mirabeau is at the very center of those who wish to see change.

"He saw *you*?" I ask in awe. "How did you get an audience with him?"

It is a great honor that Algernon has been let into this inner circle.

Algernon smiles proudly. "By offering him your services."

I stare at him. "*My* services? For what?"

Algernon takes my arm. His grip is strong and heady, and his eyes burn into mine. "I have been told that you are to draw *tableaux* of the wealthy for Dr. Curtius. Mirabeau would like a copy, so that he may use it in the pamphlets he distributes to the people. He wants to use your drawings to focus attention on the excesses of the rich and to rouse the people to action. He is willing to pay you."

I am astounded and pleased. Mirabeau wants *my* drawings for our cause? I am to provide pictures to the leader of the group that speaks out for equality? Me? Celie Rosseau? How far I have come from the girl dying by the side of the road!

"You need only remember what you have drawn for Dr. Curtius and draw it again. You can do that, can't you?" Algernon whispers, pulling me near him. "You have not forgotten, have you, Celie? You have not forgotten what we fight for? We are together still, right? A team?"

Of course I am still his, and of course I will draw for Mirabeau. Here is a chance to effect real change, to make things different for people like Maman and Papa and Jacques. Already, my fingers itch to get started.

I nod enthusiastically.

Algernon smiles, his eyes soft with feeling. "Together, we can make a real difference, Celie."

He moves toward me, and I think I will faint with anticipation. I close my eyes and tilt my head up to him, waiting. At last, a kiss. I feel his fingers softly graze my lips. Then, nothing.

"Algernon?" I say. I open my eyes to see the hesitation in his.

"Go," he says at last, and his voice is thick with emotion. "Go. Learn all you can. Draw all you can, Celie. And remember that we work for the freedom of France."

I move from the room as he bids, biting back stupid, stupid tears. Once again, I have let hope gain a foolish foothold on my heart.

∽

Three days later, the wax head has solidified, and l'Oncle removes it from its plaster casing. With l'Oncle, I smooth out the seams. My wax face now shines with a white sheen.

"I look like a ghost," I say.

"Not for long," l'Oncle tells me. "Sit here, Celie, by the light. Now, usually Manon does this. There is no one like her for matching skin tone, but as she is away, I will do the best I can."

"Besides," he adds, "I did teach her all she knows."

He turns my face right and left, picks out several different shades of beige paint and tries them on a small canvas, holding them near my skin. Finally, he nods as if satisfied and takes out a fine brush. Carefully, he paints the head, bringing a lovely look of real skin to my wax face. When he has finished, he gazes at me, and once again, matches colors, painting a rose tint onto my waxen lips.

"Tomorrow," he says, "you will visit the button maker."

"What for?" I ask, puzzled.

"Your eyes," he says.

∽

The following day, I watch as the button maker's fingers rifle through various colored marble eyes. The woman chooses some for my wax head and carefully inserts them, using the smallest of needles.

"And now you must have teeth, eh, child?" the button maker asks, when the eyes are in place. She pulls out a box, and I recoil in horror when I see all the real teeth inside.

The button maker laughs. "Do not worry, you silly girl. They come from the tooth puller. We pay him for them. They are not from the dead."

My heart stops beating so hard, and I watch as the button maker painstakingly inserts small teeth into my likeness. When she is finished, it is like looking at my own bald self.

The button maker smiles at me. "It is amazing, *n'est-ce pas?*"

☙

The next afternoon, I learn how to apply hair. L'Oncle sits beside me and directs me, showing me how to heat some beeswax and then, one by one, apply the strands. It is a tedious process, and the one I like least of all.

"Sometimes, as in the queen's case, we will use real hair she has given us, or hair from the tails of the thoroughbreds in her stable," l'Oncle explains, "but most times, we use the same horsehair we buy to stuff the models."

Of course the queen would have thoroughbred hair, while the rest of the world settles for regular old horsehair, I think to myself as I continue to work.

When the job is finished and the strands combed into place, I catch my breath with surprise. The work may be tedious, but the results are amazing. It is me, staring back at myself. How odd it feels to look at my wax head.

I laugh, and a smile flits across l'Oncle's face. Then, it is gone.

"You are not done yet," he scolds me.

I am sent next to the carpenter's, passing beggars and cripples and homeless people huddled around communal fires along the way. They shoot angry glances my way as my cart rides by, and I am shocked to suddenly realize I am now one of those who are resented.

Suddenly, a rotten tomato splatters across my face, stinging my cheek and splitting open, juices running down my cheek and the front of my gown. The crowd cheers loudly.

"That'll teach you to tax us for your pleasures," one man yells out.

"Bread," a woman calls. "We just want bread to feed our children. Is that too much to ask?"

"How can you let us starve like this?" another woman shouts.

"Next time, it will be something worse we'll throw at you," one man growls. He picks up a rock and pulls back his arm.

I duck, and the rock misses. The driver picks up speed, and we are soon safely away from the crowd. I wish I could have stopped the cart and told them that I am really one of them, that I sympathize. Now, it is too late.

At the carpenter's house, I clean the stains off my gown as best I can, shaken by the incident. I stand as the carpenter measures me, still thinking about the anger in their voices. I feel their rage. It burns inside me, too. How could they have mistaken me for one of the wealthy? Surely, they can see the difference between me and those who exploit them?

The carpenter coughs to get my attention. I try to focus as he shows me how he makes the wooden stands, how he creates wire frames and attaches them to the stand. The frames can then be bent into shape for natural curves. I am fascinated with this aspect of the waxwork-making process, and soon my thoughts about the ride are quickly forgotten. Art is again my focus.

Once my wooden and wire body is complete, l'Oncle sends me out with it to the seamstress. This time, though, with the wooden structure beside me, no one gives me a second glance. I am just a servant being sent on an errand, and I am happy for the anonymity and the clear signal that I am one of them.

The seamstress measures me yet again. Then she chooses some fabric and begins to cut. Over the next few days, I help her with the sewing of the gown and the making of stockings. When we are finished, the seamstress shows me how to put the clothes on the wooden body, and then stuff everything with horsehair until all the curves I have in real life became a part of my wooden counterpart. Finally, the seamstress sends me home with my headless body.

❧

Two days later, I am going up to my room to get ready for bed when I find l'Oncle standing beside my door. "Well, go on in," he says.

Puzzled, I enter my bedroom and find a completed wax replica of myself. I laugh with delight. It is truly me, standing there in duplicate. The artist in me is in awe of this amazing art form.

"You are a genius," I cry, and without thinking, I throw my arms about the old man.

He flinches and then relaxes and finally gives me a smile.

"*Oui*, Celie," he says, patting me awkwardly on the back. "You are right. I am a genius."

And I know that because of our art, we are now friends.

❧

Manon is home a few days later. A large, elegant carriage pulls up to 20 Boulevard du Temple, and Manon alights from it. Her hair is powdered and stacked high on her head with roses tucked into it. She wears a gown of pale blue brocade, with buttons and bows and lace at her sleeves. She looks lovely.

She comes briskly into the house, lifting her skirts and smiling when she sees me waiting for her. "You have completed your training?"

I nod.

"*C'est bien.* Then come along." Manon glides down toward the library, and I follow her. She walks over to one of the bookcases, pulling down a leather-bound book. "You read, *n'est-çe pas?*"

I hesitate, then tell her the truth. "My *papa* read, but I never got the chance to learn. Maman did not think it necessary."

"Ah, then we are two of a kind," Manon says, smiling. "Tante Marthe and l'Oncle can read, but I cannot. No matter. You will just have to learn this book as I did."

She picks up a small bell and rings it.

Tante Anne-Marie is there in a moment, giving Manon a kiss. "You are back. I have missed you."

"And I you," Manon replies, "but I can only stay a day or two, Maman. I mean to return with Celie, so she may draw some scenes for us to display."

Return where, I wonder? And will Algernon come with us? It has been two weeks since I turned my face to his, hoping for his kiss. I am almost glad to have this time to breathe and think, and yet, I do not want to be separated from him for too long.

"I must ready her," Manon says. "She cannot read. Will you have Tante Marthe read this to her? She will have to memorize it as I did."

"Memorize all that?" I cry, looking at the book Manon is holding. It is as thick as a brick. "What is it?"

"Rules of the court, five hundred pages in all," Manon tells me. "And you must know them all before we leave."

"Leave for where?" I finally ask.

"Versailles," Manon answers.

ↄ

A week later, I am packed and ready to go to the king's palace. I am torn between excitement at seeing Versailles and an uneasiness that I am about to be a part of the very lifestyle I stand against.

Just as we are about to enter the carriage, I finally see Algernon. All week I have been seeking him out and missing him. And I do not like leaving without letting him know where I am going.

He is crossing the street, his arms loaded with firewood. His eyes widen when he recognizes me, and he almost drops the logs he is carrying.

I smile as he approaches, my heart thumping wildly just to see him. But my smile quickly dies when I see the scowl on his face.

"What are you wearing?" he asks, plucking at the lace of my sleeves.

"Clothes to go to the palace," I tell him, crestfallen that he is angry with me. After all, it isn't my fault I am dressed like this.

"You're not one of them, you know," Algernon says. "You never will be."

"I know that," I say crossly, feeling as if he has punched me in the gut.

Why does he always doubt me? Does he think I like these clothes? On the contrary, they are unwieldy and constricting. And my hair has been powdered and pulled up tight on my head. Everything itches beyond belief, and I want to take my fingers and scratch my hair until it all falls down around my ears. But I have no choice, and if it means getting closer to the wealthy to draw them for Mirabeau, I am willing to endure it.

"I'm doing this for you and for Mirabeau, remember?" I remind him, with irritation. "I hope to find a way to do some drawings while I am there, and send them to you and Mirabeau for pamphlets to give to the people."

His green eyes soften at my words. "You won't forget then, Celie? You won't forget the cause or . . . ."

I will him to say "or me." But his face reddens, and he looks away.

I am impatient with this silly dance. Julia is no longer. I cannot change that.

"Or who?" I ask, deliberately baiting him.

He doesn't answer.

"Maybe I should forget," I say. "Maybe I should forget everything."

He grabs me then, and pulls me to him with a force I did not know he possessed. And he presses his lips to mine. But it is not a kind kiss. It is a desperate, angry one.

I push him roughly away. How dare he kiss me like that? As if he resents it? That is not what I longed for when I thought of us together.

"Celie," Manon calls, as she comes out from the house. "Let's go."

I turn and run from Algernon, humiliated. I fling myself into the carriage, and I do not look back once as we drive off. Instead, I sit in sullen silence, angered even more by the way I am dressed. Every time I move my head, a shower of white powder comes raining down on me, causing me to sneeze. It is the most ludicrous of ways to wear your hair. And the corset Manon forced me into this morning makes me feel as if I might throw up the sausages I had for breakfast at any moment. I burp and scowl.

Manon laughs. "You'll eat a little less at court in that contraption."

"But it will be the king's food," I snap. "Why would I want to eat less? I want to eat all the food I can. He has too much of it, anyway."

Manon reaches out suddenly and slaps me hard. "Talk like that at Versailles will get you executed."

I stare at her in shock. Manon has never done anything like this before. She has never even so much as raised her voice.

"And though I wouldn't give a second's thought to *you* being marched off to prison," Manon continues, "*I'm* not about to accompany you there. So keep your thoughts about the king to yourself, along with any other ideas that might be misconstrued as treasonous, or I'll put you back on the streets. Understand?"

I nod quickly and say nothing more, though my cheek still stings from her hand. Is everyone to be angry with me today?

Finally, Manon gives me a sympathetic look. "Your brother seemed quite upset with you when we left, Celie. Is that why you are so out of sorts?"

I do not respond. I refuse to talk about Algernon now.

We are soon at the gates of the city. A line has formed, and people sit in the middle of the road or upon their goods, waiting to be inspected and taxed. The crown collects money at the city gates: taxes on salt, tobacco, leather, iron products, soap, and wine. Royal guards search residents and visitors alike for goods being smuggled in or out. A carriage or a large cape can conceal a case of wine or a pound of soap.

I remember well entering these same gates with Algernon, just over a year ago. We had stood in line outside the gates of Paris, waiting to enter, and I had been amazed that taxes were collected just to get into the city.

"But didn't they already take taxes?" I had asked Algernon. "That's why Maman and Jacques died. We couldn't pay the taxes on the land and sow the fields."

Algernon waved his hand to quiet me, but I did not see the gesture.

"And the priest was allowed to take the first of the harvest," I had continued, oblivious, "and then, Maman had to pay the salt tax, too, even though we didn't want salt. Do we have to pay salt tax here *again*?"

A soldier had whirled upon me then. He grabbed me out of the line and began to roughly search me. I clearly remember the feeling of powerlessness as he ran his hands up and down my body, his fingers lingering where they shouldn't.

"Enough of that!" Algernon had snapped at the guard, his eyes dark with anger. "The girl's too thin for the *rags* she's wearing. She hasn't got the *room* to smuggle anything into your city."

I was relieved to have Algernon stand up for me. But then the guard turned on Algernon, poking and prodding him as if to make up for his interference. Algernon fought back, his fists cracking hard against the soldier's jaw. Then, other soldiers had descended and thrown Algernon to the ground. When they were done beating him, they had doffed their hats and apologized profusely for the "accident," laughing all the while.

As we stumbled toward the city, Algernon with a black eye, I was frightened that he would leave me behind. Why would he keep a skinny girl who opened her mouth and nearly got him killed? But I had not known about Julia then. Or about how she had perished. I did not know that because of her, he would always fight to the death before another girl died beside him, no matter who she was.

Now I tremble, thinking about going through that search once more, and how Algernon had been beaten, and how Julia had met her end, too.

"There is a long line," I say to Manon, sitting back in the carriage, my voice cracking a bit.

"We shall be through quickly," Manon says.

"But there are a lot of people waiting," I say.

"You shall see," Manon says.

In less than a minute, a guard comes over to the carriage, bypassing the line of people waiting on foot. He pulls open the door, and glares inside, his hand on his sword.

I pull myself into a ball in the corner, praying the guard will not touch me.

"We are on official royal business," I hear the coachman yell down from his seat.

The guard lets his eyes sweep over me, and then, mercifully closes the door.

"Be on your way then," he says. He waves a hand, and the other guards on duty part the long line of people. The coach rolls smoothly through.

"We won't be searched? We don't have to pay . . ." I stop, still unwilling to say the word *taxes*.

Manon shakes her head. "Not if you are of noble birth, or in one of the king's carriages on the king's business."

I look back at the ragged and cold people, waiting to leave the city for their small villages and their homes. I think of the rough way they are treated as they try to enter or leave. And the fire in my belly burns bright. I forgive Algernon his anger. Does he not have the right to be resentful, seeing me all dressed up as one of the very people he despises? Does he not have the right to be angry over the injustice he has witnessed himself? I think long and hard on this, and my determination grows to do the best drawings I have ever done for him and for Monsieur Mirabeau, and to find a way to get those drawings back to Paris to feed the flames of rebellion.

Chapter Seven

When I first glimpse Versailles, I think I am dreaming. How can anyone's home be so large, so grand? The structure in front of me, with its wide graveled avenue, 700 rooms and 2,153 windows is for one family, and one family alone. If I could draw one thing to represent wealth, I would draw Versailles. How can the king sit in this luxury, day after day, when his own subjects work themselves to death to maintain this lifestyle?

I glance over at Manon and find the lady's eyes steady upon me. I want to ask her what she thinks of Versailles, if she had been as affronted at its grandeur and size the first time she saw it. But I suspect that Manon will not answer, so I keep the question to myself and do my best to swallow my incredulity.

When the carriage finally comes to a stop, a servant dressed entirely in blue, with quarter-inch silver buttons, white lace, and silk stockings, his hair powdered and tied neatly back with a thin blue velvet ribbon, opens the door. As if she has been born to it, Manon descends from the carriage.

I rise, too, and totter precariously at the edge of the vehicle, cursing my top-heavy hair and wide skirts. I just manage to climb from the carriage without falling face first.

The servant bows, and Manon takes off, walking sedately across the courtyard and toward the back of the palace.

"Aren't we going in?" I ask, following her.

Manon smiles slightly. "*Non*, Celie. The king's sister tends to stay at the *Petit Trianon*, a smaller palace on the grounds here, or in her home by the gates on the road from Paris. I left Madame Élisabeth last at the Trianon, so I thought we would go there first.

But even if she is not there, I thought you might enjoy seeing the grounds of Versailles. Study them closely. I may have you draw them later for a display at the museum."

We round the corner of the palace and come into the gardens. I gaze out at the wide vista of green lawns, ornamental trees, and fountains. I have never seen anything so lovely. The grass seems to stretch on for miles, with trees lining each side of the pathways. Directly in front of me, a large fountain spouts out arcs of water, a statue of Apollo rising from the middle, four horses dragging his chariot from the depths, their mouths open, straining as if they bear a tremendous weight. Two tritons announce Apollo's arrival as dolphins swim beside him. The middle arc of water forms a perfect *fleur-de-lis*, the symbol of the French royal family. Beyond the fountain lies an enormous canal, upon which float brightly painted gondolas. Peacocks strut about, screeching their odd cry of mating.

Women stroll the grounds, parasols raised to guard their white skin against the early spring sunshine. Men accompany them, their white powdered wigged heads tilted just so, listening intently to their companions' conversation even as their eyes sweep the gardens back and forth, taking note of everyone else who is out and about. A gentle breeze ruffles the newly sprouted leaves of the trees.

"Ahem." Manon coughs. She moves her hands so they rest lightly on the large hoops of her skirt. I understand. Now is the time to remember the rules of the court.

I follow Manon's lead and rest my hands as Manon has done. Daintily, I stroll along, remembering from the book that was read to me that when you walk, you are to look as if you are gliding, not taking a step. I don't see how the women manage it, as the small pebbles of the pathway dig into my silk slippers. I want to grimace, to hop up and down and swear when a stone tears into my instep. But instead, I bite my lip and carry on beside

Manon. The whole charade is the most ridiculous thing I've ever encountered.

We pass couple after couple. Occasionally, Manon coughs slightly, reminding me to curtsy deeply when we encounter someone of noble blood, rising only when our betters have passed.

I try to stay steady, but I am busy noting all the dresses and coats, the cut and style of each, the colors, and the decorations that trim them. The women's bodices glow with the red of rubies and the flash of diamonds. The men's jackets have silver threads running through them. The richness of the cloth makes my head spin.

If a servant passes us, Manon nods slightly, and the servant always returns the nod, even if they are carrying trays of food and drink or hats and riding gear.

"A very deep curtsy, if you please," Manon suddenly instructs me.

I look ahead and am startled to see the Comte d'Artois heading toward us with two elaborately dressed companions: a lovely lady in a gold brocade gown with buckled shoes and real silk stockings, and a man with a dark green waistcoat and silver buttons. Annoyance burns through me at the Comte strolling so carefree through such beautiful gardens. I do not want to bow to this man, and so, I hesitate.

"I will pay you half my takings if you do as I have asked," Manon whispers.

Instantly, I am in a curtsy so deep, I am afraid I will need someone to help me up. Already I am thinking of what Algernon and I could buy with those coins. Out of the corner of my eye, I see the sides of Manon's lips curl up in amusement.

"Monsieur le Comte," Manon says, rising and presenting once more an implacable face.

"Mademoiselle Manon," the Comte d'Artois says. "How pleasant to see you."

I rise from my curtsy, too, and raise my eyes to meet the Comte's.

He steps back, shock written on his face.

"So nice to see you again, Monsieur le Comte," I say, keeping my face agreeable though my cheeks ache with the effort of it.

"What a pretty girl," the lady with the Comte says.

"Pretty girl? That little urchin gave me this." The Comte pulls down the lace at his collar to show his friends a white scar on his neck, and I have to swallow a grimace. Though I do not like the man, I did not mean to mar him, and again, I am ashamed of having resorted to violence when wit is a better game.

"The Comte has made a bet that I will be unable to bring the girl into line," Manon says.

"It seems that you have lost then, Monsieur le Comte," the lady with the Comte says, "for the girl curtsies and smiles quite prettily."

"And so she does," the man beside them agrees. "How much did you wager?"

"Our bet was for one thousand *livres. Oui,* Monsieur le Comte?" Manon answers.

My head spins with the thought of one half of one thousand *livres.* It is difficult for me to even imagine that much money. But what I can envision is Algernon's pleasure. With half of one thousand *livres,* we would never need worry about food or shelter again. And maybe we would have time for other things, such as rebellion and romance.

I see us living on a little plot of land, growing our own food, keeping our own cottage, writing pamphlets, holding meetings. I am heady with these ideas, and determined to win now that I am to share in the profit.

The Comte scowls. "The bet was that she would behave properly, not that you could dress her correctly. In your business, that would be too easy a task. The question is, have you truly contained her wild nature? And for that, Mademoiselle Manon, we shall have to give the urchin time to prove herself one way or another."

The dream of Algernon's arms around me evaporates with his words.

"But I've just been nice to you, you toad," I bark out before I can stop myself.

The Comte looks at me as if stunned. "Is that any way to speak to the king's brother?" He smiles wickedly. "Perhaps I shall win the bet after all."

The lady and gentleman with the Comte laugh with him, reducing me to the fool. I have let my anger get the best of me yet again.

But Manon only smiles. "We shall see, *monsieur*. We shall see."

And with that, the Comte passes us by, the elegant lady and gentleman going with him, leaving Manon and me deep in another curtsy, my eyes on the ground, my cheeks burning with shame. My head pounds, and my nails bite into the palm of my hand. I curse my loud mouth.

I will prove that man wrong, and I will have that money for Algernon and me if it is the last thing I do.

⟡

The Petit Trianon is a solid block of a palace with large windows and columns. A broad portico surrounds the chateau. There were so many people walking the garden paths, and here, even more sit on benches.

"How many people *live* here?" I ask, my head spinning.

"The king's family, of course, and all their servants," Manon says. "And thousands of courtiers live nearby. They come daily so that they may gain favor with the king."

"Thousands?" I echo. It is one thing to think that the king ignores the plight of the poor, but I cannot comprehend how thousands of people can do the same. Have they not seen what is happening beyond these walls?

Manon nods. "That book you spent so much time memorizing was written to keep these courtiers' minds from plotting against the king while they are here."

"That's clever," I say bitterly, thinking of the king spending his time writing decrees to keep his throne safe from the hands of those who would wrest it from him, rather than concentrating on matters of state.

"Mmm," Manon says. "Do you think so? If everyone is so busy worrying about following these rules, then when is there time to do the work of the country?"

I pause. I had not considered that even the king's men are not working on the problems of France. "Is that why so many people are starving?"

"Perhaps," Manon says. "Or perhaps it was just a poor harvest?"

"Well, which is it?" I ask, irritated by Manon's evasiveness.

Manon smiles slightly. "You must decide that yourself, Celie."

I frown. What does she *think*? Is she for the king, or against him?

But Manon is already far ahead of me on the path, and I have to hurry to catch up, hoping I do not trip over my wide skirts as I run lightly along. We approach a small door hidden around a corner of the Petit Trianon. A servant stands at attention by it. He bows when he sees Manon and opens the door for us.

We enter a windowless corridor fitted with rounded ceilings, crowded with servants rushing here and there. I sigh. Unfortunately, *this* feels more like where we belong. The place smells of hot breath and bodies packed too closely together.

I follow Manon up four flights of stairs. My corset digs into my sides, making me stop several times to catch my breath, and I have to keep turning to get my wide *pannier* hoopskirt up the stairs. I almost laugh as I imagine trying to live on the streets in these contraptions. Every criminal would be caught easily, as they could never run away.

At last, we reach the very top. Manon walks down another narrow corridor until we are in front of an open door. We enter a room with a single bed and dresser.

"You are here," Manon says. "I am right across the hall."

"Should I go back down and get our things?" I ask, though I am dreading climbing up all those stairs again.

"*Non*," Manon says. "Someone will bring our bags along shortly. I will go to Madame Élisabeth first, and then come back for you if she gives me permission to present you to her today."

I walk into my new bedroom. It isn't half as nice as the room I have at Manon's. There is a looking glass and a wardrobe for my dresses, but the bed is narrow and the blankets thin. And there is only a very small fireplace, and a tiny window. Still, it is far better than the alley at the Palais-Royal.

I wonder what Algernon is doing now. Is he moving exhibits in the museum? Is he running errands for l'Oncle? Is he thinking of me now as I am thinking of him? Does he regret kissing me the way he did? Does he regret kissing me at all? I take a deep breath and firmly put thoughts of Algernon aside. I have work to do here, places and people to memorize and recall. I cannot let thoughts of Algernon distract me.

There is a knock on my slightly open door. A little boy dressed in the blue livery of the king stands there, my valise by his side. For a moment, I believe he is my brother Jacques brought back to life, and my breath leaves me.

Then the little boy bows to me, and reality hits me, hard. Of course he is not my brother. My brother is dead.

I sit down stiffly on the bed. I think of Jacques's wide smile and his dancing brown eyes, the way he was always tripping over the water pail in our house when he ran in from the fields, or breaking the crockery when he dug in to eat supper. And I am confronted once more with the fact that I will never see my brother alive again.

"*Mademoiselle*," the boy says, "are you all right?"

I almost laugh. This little boy is so formal—not at all like Jacques was.

"How old are you?" I ask, my voice cracking with suppressed emotion.

The boy frowns. "Eight, not that it's any of your business."

He *is* Jacques's age, though—or Jacques's age, should my brother have lived. Once again, his loss scrapes unmercifully at my heart.

"What is your name?" I ask.

If I am to be alone here, I would like to make a friend who reminds me of my brother. Though the memories might hurt, keeping them alive is important. I never want to forget my brother, or my mother and father.

"Jean-Louis," he replies. He tries to brush past me with my suitcase. But the valise is heavy, and he stumbles.

"Here," I say, standing. "Let me help you."

"*Non*," Jean-Louis cries, his face whitening. "My *papa* is one of the porters, and he will be angry if I do not carry the luggage myself. It is what I am paid for."

"All right," I say, "if you wish. Though no one can see you in my room if I close the door."

Jean-Louis looks at me uncertainly. I grab his momentary hesitation to shut the door firmly. Then I bend down and take one end of the suitcase. Together, we lift the valise across the room, nearer to the bed.

"*Merci*," Jean-Louis says as we set the bag down.

He looks up at me. "That was heavy. What have you got in there?"

I laugh. "Drawing paper, pencils, brushes, paints, some underthings, and my one other dress."

"That's all?" Jean-Louis asks, and he looks completely crestfallen.

"The paints are heavy," I lie.

Jean-Louis nods solemnly. "It took all my strength to get them up the stairs."

"You did a fine job," I assure him.

There is a heavy knocking on the door.

Jean-Louis turns frightened eyes on me.

"Come in," I say.

Another porter is standing there. "What is taking you so long, Jean-Louis?" he demands.

Jean-Louis pales.

"I'm sorry," I say, stepping in. "He was helping me with my suitcase."

"*Oui*, and that is all he is to do," the porter sniffs angrily. "There are other more important people he must see to. Hurry now, Jean-Louis. *Vite. Vite.* Or I will see you replaced."

He claps his hands, and Jean-Louis goes running from the room, terrified.

I stare at this man, appalled. I expected unkind behavior from the royals, but from one of their staff?

"Was that necessary?" I ask. "To frighten him like that?"

The porter gives me a contemptuous look. "I am the man in charge of the porters. It is my job on the line if he is not quick enough. If the boy cannot perform, there are others waiting to take his job. I cannot afford to coddle him."

Manon comes in then. "Ah, your bags are here. Good. Freshen up now. Madame Élisabeth will see you straightaway."

The porter bows slightly to Manon, who nods at him. Then he goes to the door, looking back once at me.

I catch his look, and see in his eyes a bit of shame. But I know that he is right. In this world we live in, we all must fight for a chance to live and eat.

"Celie?" Manon says, bringing me out of my thoughts. "Come along."

And now I, too, must hurry to respond to a royal desire. So I restore the wisps of hair that have come undone, pat down the wrinkles in my dress, and follow Manon toward the innermost part of the palace.

૯ૐ

We descend two flights of stairs. Manon scratches lightly upon the door, using only her fingertips as the etiquette book demands.

I am about to walk into one of the rooms belonging to the sister of the king of France. My hands shake, and my mouth is suddenly dry. I have only felt frightened like this once before—in the weeks I spent stumbling my way toward Paris after Maman's and Jacques's deaths. It is a feeling I do not like. And why, after all, should I be scared of royals? They are just people.

Still, this rationalization does not eliminate the feeling, and I tremble like leaves in the wind as an usher swings the door open. Immediately, I am blinded with sparks of light and gold. When at last my eyes adjust to the brilliance of the room, I see a young woman sitting at a writing desk, surrounded by seven thin, gray dogs.

In contrast to the women and men I have seen walking the gardens of Versailles, this woman is dressed plainly, only a small bit of lace at her sleeves and no jewelry around her neck. Her light hair is twisted into a bun and pulled back from a clear face. She turns, and her blue eyes light up on seeing me,

"Ah, you have brought her," she cries. "Come in, child. Come in."

I walk slowly toward her, remembering to keep my back straight, my chin high. But my senses are so overwhelmed that I feel I might faint. Gold glitters from the woodwork. Life-size paintings adorn the walls. Rich brocades decorate the windows and chairs. Mirrors reflect the sunshine from tall windows. Wallpaper, rich in floral decoration, runs from floor to ceiling. The colors, the light, the grandeur of the furnishings all swirl about me, filling my senses to the point of explosion. Yet when I reach the lady, I somehow manage to drop into a curtsy so perfect, I know Manon will be proud of me.

"Rise, child," Madame Élisabeth commands.

I stand and find Madame Élisabeth regarding me frankly as she strokes the head of one of her dogs. "I hear you have some very special talents."

I don't know what to say. If I respond *oui*, it will sound like bragging. I stand there, frozen.

Madame Élisabeth lets out a light laugh. "Have I scared her, Manon?"

Manon glides up to me. "I am sure she is just a bit overwhelmed, *madame*."

I feel something cold and wet on my hand, and I jump. Then I realize that one of Madame Élisabeth's dogs has nuzzled up against me. Without thinking, I bend over and stroke the animal. The dog licks my hand, and I laugh merrily, reminded of Algernon and his strays.

"Ah, you are a dog lover, *n'est-çe pas?*" Madame Élisabeth asks. "Then, Celie, you and I shall be good friends, for I adore them."

With Madame Élisabeth's kind words, my earlier fear seems to fly right out one of the large windows of the room, and I am relieved to have it gone.

"What is his name?" I ask her.

"*Her* name is Daphné," Madame Élisabeth corrects. "And she likes you."

I smile at this woman. "I like her, too."

"Come, Celie," Manon says. "Let us not waste Madame Élisabeth's valuable time. We must show her what you can do. Take a moment to look at the room."

I straighten and glance about me. How am I to remember all these details?

"Celie," Manon says. She points to a table near Madame Élisabeth. "Please sit when you are ready. You will draw without looking up. Do you understand?"

She gives me a look that lets me know that she is well aware of the nervousness I feel. The look steadies me. I have been brought to do this, and so I must do it right—for Manon's sake, and for Algernon's.

I take a deep breath and begin to look about the room. It will not be hard to do if I only take in one thing at a time, if I can just forget where I actually am. How is this so different from drawing at the Palais-Royal, or sketching in the dirt after scouting out a wealthy family's parlor? More elaborate? Maybe. More detailed? Definitely. But I am good. I know I can handle this.

Confidence fills me. I continue to gaze about the room, turning slowly in a circle, looking at table, chair, mirror, curtains, fireplace, wallpaper, paintings. At last, I am satisfied; I can sense it imprinted on my mind. So I take my place at the table, and begin to draw.

As time goes by, I am dimly aware of people coming and going, and of someone looking over my shoulder several times. I hear the clinking of china and smell the sweet scent of warm bread. But I do not look up, nor stop what I am doing. My fingers fly across the paper. My mind dances with the images I have seen down to the very last detail—a tiny rose on the tenth chair in the room, the thin thread running through the curtains that move gently in the spring breeze, the scratch marks at the bottom of the legs of the table at which Madame Élisabeth sits.

Hours later, I am finally finished. I sit back and rub my eyes, shrugging my shoulders to relieve the tension in them. The brightness has faded from the room, leaving much of it in shadows.

"You are done?"

I look up.

Madame Élisabeth is standing next to me. "May I see?"

I nod.

Madame Élisabeth picks up the drawing and slowly looks around the room, her eye moving from drawing to room and back again.

"Amazing," she finally whispers. "Such talent you have, child."

I grow warm from Madame Élisabeth's praise.

"She will teach you all she knows," Manon says.

Madame Élisabeth laughs lightly. "She may show me all she knows, but I highly doubt I will learn it, Manon. Memorizing such as this is rare, not a thing to be taught. Still, I will value having her as a drawing tutor, and I can see why she is such a valuable asset to your museum. She will draw many scenes here for you to display in Paris."

She turns to me, her eyes warm. "But now, child, it is way past teatime, and you did not move from your spot. Come have a pastry and some hot chocolate."

I look over at Manon, who inclines her head. I follow Madame Élisabeth to a small table on which lie the remnants of food and drink.

"Please clear this, and lay a new place," Madame Élisabeth orders.

Three servants in the room scurry about, picking up the dirty plates and used cups. Another servant puts down a clean plate for me, and a fourth delivers a tray of fresh, hot pastries. Another brings a pot of hot liquid, and a sixth pours it. After each has finished their task, they curtsy to Madame Élisabeth. My head swims as the servants swirl about us. There are so many of them!

"Hot chocolate is the queen's favorite," Madame Élisabeth tells me. "She has it for breakfast every day. Do you like it?"

I take a sip of the dark brown drink. I have never had hot chocolate, and the sweet, smooth, unusual flavor of it swims about my mouth.

"I like it very much, *madame*," I say, enchanted by the taste. "I would have it for breakfast every day, too, if I could."

"A pastry?" Madame Élisabeth smiles, holding out a plate of croissants.

The roll melts in my mouth. I have never tasted a croissant so full of butter. I take my time, taking a bite of the pastry and then drinking a sip of the chocolate.

But even though I wish to make the moment continue forever, at last all the chocolate is gone, and there isn't a flake of croissant remaining on the plate.

Madame Élisabeth stands up. "I shall see you tomorrow afternoon, then."

Manon signals to me to get up from my seat. Together, we drop into a curtsy as Madame Élisabeth leaves the room.

When Manon rises, she smiles at me. "You did well, Celie. I am pleased."

Glad of this, I follow Manon back up the stairs to our rooms. But when she opens my door and I see the plainness and the cramped space of it, I am appalled at how easily I have been swept up by Madame Élisabeth's charm and the ease of her world. And I remind myself never to forget that the lifestyle of Madame Élisabeth is for Madame Élisabeth and her family alone, and that the rest of France lives like this—or worse.

Chapter Eight

The following morning, when we arrive at Madame Élisabeth's apartments, we find the king's sister on her knees, praying. I am surprised to see this, as Algernon has told me the whole court is ungodly and decadent.

"*Bonjour,*" Madame Élisabeth says. Her ladies-in-waiting hurry to help her rise.

Manon and I curtsy.

"I thought today we would go outside and do some drawing," Madame Élisabeth suggests. "The walk might give Celie some ideas for a new royal scene in your museum."

Manon smiles. "That is very kind, Madame Élisabeth. Did you have anywhere in mind?"

"I thought the grotto might be cool and pleasant," Madame Élisabeth says. "But we could stop at the *Petit Hameau* first, as Celie is an animal lover."

She smiles at me, then turns to her servants. "Have food brought to us at the grotto in two hours' time. And bring my drawing items with me now."

Three servants bow and leave the room. Three more curtsy and gather up Madame Élisabeth's drawing tools. Manon and I follow Madame Élisabeth and her ladies-in-waiting outside into the bright sunshine. Behind us, the servants totter with their arms full of easels, paper, paints, and brushes. Madame Élisabeth's dogs scamper about. Daphné nudges me before running to join the others as they nose about the palace grounds.

As we make our way through the gardens of Versailles, courtiers and ladies walk the paths around us, each curtsying or bowing deeply to Madame Élisabeth and her ladies-in-waiting, and Manon and I curtsying to them. It makes our walk a very long and tedious process. But at last we reach what seems to be a small village, with a thatched cottage and several farm outbuildings. In a meadow further away, sheep and cows graze.

I am enchanted. I have never seen a farm so clean or peaceful looking. *"Is this where they collect milk and cheese for the palace?"*

Madame Élisabeth's ladies-in-waiting giggle.

Madame Élisabeth smiles. *"Non, ma petite.* This farm was designed especially for the queen. She likes to come here and pretend she is a commoner."

"The queen thinks *this* is what a French farm looks like?" I say, laughing along with the others at the joke. "If she really wants to live like a commoner, she should add missing thatch to the roof, or have the doors hanging half open because no French farmer can afford the nails to fix them, and . . . ."

I stop when I see the dismay in Madame Élisabeth's eyes and the anger in Manon's, and I realize that I've let my mouth run on.

"Sorry," I mumble.

The door to the cottage suddenly opens, and five women in white muslin dresses spill out. They run to the distant meadow and begin picking wildflowers. When they have gathered armfuls, they sit upon the ground and begin weaving them in their hair, laughing. One of the women looks toward us and waves merrily.

"Ah," Madame Élisabeth says. "I did not know the queen would be here."

I stare at the woman dressed as the others. This is the queen? Marie Antoinette? This woman who is prancing about and clapping her hands above her head, like a gypsy dancer?

"Élisabeth!" the queen calls. "We are to picnic today. Come eat with us."

"Shall we join them, *madame?"* one of the ladies-in-waiting asks, her face lit up with anticipation.

Madame Élisabeth shakes her head. "I think not. Let us go to the grotto instead. I would prefer to do some drawing there. I am sorry, Celie. I will bring you to the Petit Hameau another time, so that you may see the sheep and cows."

I am disappointed not to see Marie Antoinette up close, but I am not sorry we have come. I am already thinking about drawing the scene for Mirabeau—a queen dancing about and pretending to be a commoner, while her subjects—true commoners—go hungry. Surely a drawing such as that will encourage the people to stand up to their king, and force him to pay attention to their plight.

Now the question is—how do I get my hands on some drawing paper without Manon noticing? And even more importantly, how do I get my drawings to Algernon?

☙

My dilemma is solved for me one morning several weeks later, when a servant comes to find me. "Mademoiselle Manon wishes to see you," she tells me.

I go and find Manon sitting with the man who reads her letters to her. Manon looks up as I enter, and holds out a small piece of paper. "It seems your accomplice in crime would like to communicate with you."

I look down at the scrap of paper. On it is nothing but a question mark, and though the mark is crude, I know Algernon's hand has drawn it. I can almost see him as he bends over the paper, his brown hair falling into his eyes. My breath catches as I gaze at it, and I am suddenly homesick for him and for Paris.

While it is nice at Versailles, I have let my commitment to change languish. Algernon must be wondering by now if I have given up our fight and succumbed to the pleasures of an easy life. Thinking that maybe he was right to wish me to focus on the cause makes me feel guilty. I cannot let him down—nor my own family.

"L'Oncle says Algernon wished you to receive this," Manon says. "Tell me, Celie, you are not plotting anything while you are here, are you? And do not lie to me. There is talk all over France of rebellion, and I refuse to be a part of it. Nor will I have my apprentices involved, either."

I shake my head, but my mind is racing. If I am smart, I can work this to my advantage. "I promised Algernon I would write to him."

I see Manon's eyes narrow and curse my own stupidity. I can't write to Algernon, for Algernon can't read, and I can't write.

"I mean that I promised to send him some drawings, so that he might see where I was and how things are here," I stammer out.

Again, Manon's head lifts as if she senses some untruth. I know I am walking on shaky ground. If Manon suspects that I am planning on sending pictures so that Algernon and Mirabeau can use them in their pamphlets for their crusade to force the king to be more reasonable in his spending and lavishness, I will be trundled back to Paris and be out on the streets faster than Algernon can lift a few coins from a woman's *porte-monnaie*. I steady myself.

"Algernon worries about me and about the care I receive," I say. "I would like to draw him a picture or two so that I may ease his mind."

Manon scowls. "It seems to me he has always been more interested in your abilities than your welfare."

I bite my tongue to stop myself from responding, *As are you.* Too much is riding on Manon's answer. If Manon says *non*, I will have to resort to stealing paper and still will have no way to send my drawings to Algernon.

"Fine," Manon finally says, "but it will be on your own time, and I will give you only one piece of my parchment paper. It is expensive. If you ruin it, it will be your problem, not mine."

I try to keep the glow of satisfaction I feel from spreading to my face. I have convinced Manon. And that is not an easy task.

∽

The next day, Madame Élisabeth decides that once more, we will do our drawing out of doors. The day is warm for May, and a steady breeze blows our dresses about. We walk the short path toward the large canal that leads to the great palace of Versailles. There, near the water, we find servants scurrying back and forth, and crowds of brilliantly dressed courtiers gathering.

"What is happening here?" Madame Élisabeth calls to one of the servants.

The woman curtsies low to Madame Élisabeth. "There is to be a naval battle on the water today. Lunch is to be served outside for everyone."

"A naval battle?" I ask, my heart racing. "Are we at war?"

I have heard no rumors of an attack. And how would an enemy's ships sail to Versailles, which is landlocked? It makes no sense.

Madame Élisabeth laughs. "*Non, ma petite.* Occasionally my brother re-enacts a famous naval battle out on these waters for the court's viewing pleasure. Perhaps we could watch. Would you like that?"

"Oh, *oui*," I say at once, for Madame Élisabeth does not often vary her schedule.

"Then come," Madame Élisabeth says. "Let us find a spot from which we may view the proceedings."

I feel a thrill of anticipation. I am about to see some court entertainment.

We come upon a gathering of gilt chairs surrounding two larger throne-like seats. A tent has been erected above the furniture to provide shade from the late spring sun. Madame Élisabeth motions for Manon and me to stand behind her. Then she moves forward and seats herself gracefully on one of the smaller gilt chairs.

I strain to look around the gathering crowds. Already I can see that two naval ships have been launched out onto the water. They are certainly not as large as the military ships I have seen in Paris, but still, they look exactly like them in all their detail. Actors, dressed as sailors, clamber about the vessels.

There is a commotion in the crowd, and Manon touches my hand, indicating that we should curtsy. I follow her lead and watch through lowered lashes as the rest of the crowd drops into bows and curtsies, like a wave sweeping the shore.

And then the king and queen are passing by, and my thoughts tumble about as I try to memorize every detail of our sovereigns. The king is surprisingly ugly—short and rotund, with an unremarkable chin and squinty eyes. His waistcoat strains against his belly, but it is made of fine cloth. His shoes are polished, and fitted with diamond buckles. The king peers about, looking rather bored, as if this is the last place in the world he wants to be.

The queen, on the other hand, is beautifully and regally dressed in pale yellow silk, trimmed with buttons of pearls in the shape of daisies, and a white satin stomacher. Her light hair is piled high. At the very top of her elaborate tresses, rests a model naval ship, identical in every detail to the ships that are lying in the waters of the canal. Her young face is beaming with pleasure as she says *bonjour* to person after person, whispering a quick confidence to one and laughing slightly with another.

When the king and queen have passed, I start to rise, but Manon stays me with a hand, for behind the king and queen come their children. I look at them with curiosity, for the princess is only a few years younger than I am. She is clothed much like the queen, her dress a light pink, a necklace of rubies and diamonds around her neck. Holding her hand is her youngest brother, age eight, skipping along as if he has not a care in the world. Ringlets of gold circle his head, and his eyes dance with excitement. Behind his brother and sister comes the heir to the throne, Louis-Joseph, looking tired but excited. He has been sick of late, battling tuberculosis. He walks slowly, but still I feel some sense of awe to get a glimpse of the boy who will be king.

Again I go to rise when the royal children have passed, and again Manon stays me as the companions to the children follow behind.

"My legs are shaking," I say. "Can't I stand up just for a second?"

"*Non*," Manon says. "Not until the entire royal family has gone by."

At that moment there is a parting of the crowd, and the Comte d'Artois strolls past. He pauses for a moment when he sees me, and then walks on without acknowledging us. I have to resist the urge to stick out a foot and trip him.

At last, we rise, my legs wobbly from the effort of maintaining a curtsy for so long. The royal family are all seated near the canal: the king and queen, their children, Madame Élisabeth, and the Comte d'Artois.

"The royal family sitting together would make a wonderful exhibit at the museum," I say to Manon. "Would you like me to draw it, to send to l'Oncle?"

Manon smiles. "Spoken like a good apprentice."

From her drawing bag, Manon hands me a piece of parchment paper, a board, and a pencil as the battle out on the water begins. The ships sail into position. The roar of guns and cannons echoes out across the water. The crowds press closer to the banks of the canal, straining to watch the battle. My hand flies across the paper.

The crowd claps as the French ship's cannon rips into its enemy counterpart. I move from Manon to get a better view, ducking under one man's arm, stepping on another lady's long dress, apologizing as I go.

But I stop abruptly when I spot Jean-Louis standing just behind the crowd. His face is tear-stained. What can he be crying about?

"Are you not enjoying the entertainment?" I ask him when I reach him.

"I am in trouble, Celie," he wails. "Papa has been ill with fever this past week, and he asked me to do his job so that no one will notice. I was to deliver the marquis de Lafayette's luggage to his room, but it is locked. And I cannot get in. We could be let go if I cannot find a way to deliver the marquis's suitcase to him, and my *papa* and I will go hungry again, just like we did before Papa got this job."

I hesitate. I know Manon will not approve. But I know what it means to be hungry and without a home.

"Come, Jean-Louis, show me to the door," I say, making up my mind, and hoping I will not come to regret it.

I follow Jean-Louis up the stairs inside the Petit Trianon until we stand in front of a large, elaborately decorated door painted in gold leaf. Beside the door sits the marquis's luggage.

"Do you really think you can unlock it?" Jean-Louis asks.

I set down my pencil and drawing board and examine the lock closely. It is more complicated than other locks I have seen. I take one of the pins from my hair, and a large piece comes tumbling down, showering us both with powder.

"Sorry," I mutter as I bend down to look once more at the lock. The mechanism inside is fairly complicated. I insert my hairpin, carefully twisting it the way Algernon has taught me. I listen as the tumblers inside make a slight clicking sound. Then I rise and twist the handle of the door. Still locked.

"Are you sure this is the right room, Jean-Louis?" I ask.

He nods, tears coming to his eyes again.

"Stop crying," I tell him. "Crying never helps anything."

I bend back over the lock. "I don't know why someone would lock up an empty guest room so tightly."

"The king does it," Jean-Louis says, sniffling and wiping his nose. "He loves locks. He is always installing locks he makes himself on the doors to empty rooms around the palaces."

"Then why don't you just go ask him for the key?" I ask in exasperation, as once more the door will not open.

Jean-Louis's eyes widen. "I cannot just go up and ask the king for a key."

"Why not?" I snap, as my third attempt does not unlock the door, either. I am getting anxious. It won't be long before Manon notices my absence. "Especially if he is the one who put the lock on here in the first place."

"It is for us to figure out," Jean-Louis says. "The king wishes to become a master locksmith, and so, he practices on his servants. It is a game to him."

I straighten up and stare at Jean-Louis. "A game?"

Jean-Louis nods. "He *wants* us to try and unlock it. He is trying to build a lock that no one can undo. We must each try four times, and only then, can we go to the king's man and ask for help. But if we are late doing our duties, we take the blame."

At this, Jean-Louis begins to cry again. "This is the second time this has happened to me. If I don't have the luggage in the room by the time the entertainment is over, and the marquis comes to change his clothes, I will be let go."

Jean-Louis's words roar in my ears. The injustice of it all decides me. If it takes all day, I will unlock this room. I bend down over the lock, listening carefully as I move the hairpin back and forth.

From outside, the sound of cheering and the roar of guns grow louder. Sweat drips down my face and gathers in my armpits. But at last, I hear the small clicking noises that indicate that the lock is coming undone. Two more flicks of my wrist and I stand, wiping my brow. Then I put out a hand, and open the door. Jean-Louis starts crying again. But this time, I assume, it is with relief.

 confident that ❧

When I finally arrive back at the canal, the naval battle is ending with the enemy ship sunk, and the actors who have played its sailors splashing around and crying for help. The queen claps and laughs, obviously delighted with the spectacle. The courtiers and servants join in the jubilation.

I do not applaud, and I see Manon frown at me. I don't care. The naval battle has probably cost thousands of *livres* to create. And watching it after just unlocking a door that the king has secured at random for his strange hobby piques my anger.

I am furious that the king spends his time making locks rather than concentrating on running his country fairly. How can I have been here these past few weeks and done nothing to help out our cause?

I have finished my drawing for Manon, and I have not started anything to show the royals' lavish lifestyle. At least in this, I can get busy.

I take out the extra piece of parchment Manon has given me and begin to draw a second sketch of the naval battle. I have waited too long to go back to the Petit Hameau and draw there. The scene before me is wild in its excesses. It should be enough to incite a response in the people of Paris. I sit upon the banks of the canal as the battle draws to its finale, and sketch away. I draw the king and queen, chatting casually with their courtiers, the day bright with sunshine as the captain of the French ship stands at the bow of his replica and makes a final speech of heroic proportions. At length, a shadow falls across my drawing.

"You have done too much, Celie." Manon's voice is sharp. "We do not have the room to recreate the naval battle itself in our space at Le Salon de Cire."

Nor would you if you could, I think bitterly. She is unwilling to risk the wrath of the royals, and so she would never display anything so controversial. Silently, I hand up the first finished drawing to Manon, who looks it over. The drawing is a bland one, showing the king and queen sitting quietly and regally.

"Very good, but why then are you drawing a second piece?" she asks.

"For Algernon," I say, as I continue to sketch. The canal and the ships are finished. The king and queen are sketched in. I can finish the detail later. I begin outlining the other spectators, trying to quickly capture it all in my mind, for the entertainment is drawing to a close.

"Wouldn't it be more appropriate for you to sketch the quarters in which you are living, since your criminal companion is so concerned about your welfare?" Manon asks.

My hand stops sketching for a moment. "Algernon loves naval battles. I thought to let him see how much I am enjoying the entertainments at court."

"I am not sure this is the appropriate picture to be sending back to Paris," Manon says, her voice steady but determined. "A less extravagant one would be more to your friend's liking, I think."

Manon is aware of the dangers in conveying such a drawing to someone outside the court system. She knows it would display to the poor all the senseless waste of the court. Her words make my blood boil.

"I am working for you, as you wished. Isn't that enough? Will you now tell me what I may or may not draw, too?" I snap.

There is a loud roar from the crowd. The entertainment has come to a close.

The king rises abruptly. Everyone grows quiet, dropping swiftly into a deep bow or curtsy. I rise and curtsy, too, but my pulse pounds in my ears as the king passes me. He looks hot and tired, even though he sat during the performance with a servant fanning his face.

I hate him. I hate them all, sitting there so smugly, spending money as if there was as much of it in France as water droplets in the canal before us. I hate Manon for keeping her mouth shut and letting this excess continue while others starve. She has the means to let the people know what happens here, yet she will not use it.

I am disappointed in myself, in how I have wasted these past few weeks simply teaching Madame Élisabeth and drawing for l'Oncle's insipid exhibits back in Paris. I should have been advancing the cause of the people.

I spy Jean-Louis in the crowd, his head almost to his knees as he honors the very man who has almost lost him his job. I am tired of doing nothing that might poke or prod this king into action. And then, suddenly, I know what I can do.

I smile, imagining Algernon laughing with delight over my new idea. It will be great fun for me, and it will teach this king a lesson, even if it is only in a small way. At least, it will be something.

The Comte d'Artois pauses by me. "Have you seen something funny?"

"She has just enjoyed the entertainment, Monsieur le Comte," Manon answers smoothly. "She smiles because it has pleased her to see it."

"I believe the girl can speak herself, Mademoiselle Manon," the Comte snaps. "You forget I know just what kind of tongue she holds in that pretty head of hers."

"A tongue that has grown civil and ladylike," Manon answers.

"Or perhaps she has a serpent's tongue," the Comte replies, "smiling pleasantly, but forking her tongue with insolence when no one is looking,"

"She has been here going on three weeks now, *monsieur*," Manon says, "and she is well-received. Your sister has grown quite fond of her."

The Comte snorts. "My sister is a fool. She trusts everyone. But you see, I know better, for storm clouds are gathering even as we speak. And it is urchins like this one here who are bringing them together."

My face grows hot, as my thoughts slide unbidden to the drawing that even now I hold in my sweaty hands.

"I will be watching you, girl," the Comte says, his voice low and heavy with threat. "I will be watching you very closely."

"Watch her as closely as you like, Monsieur le Comte," Manon says, smiling. "You will find here only a loyal subject who honors her king and queen."

As the Comte walks away, Manon turns to face me. She takes my half-finished drawing from my hand. "I will send this along, the way it currently is. But do not prove me wrong in what I have said to the Comte, Celie, or you shall have me to deal with. And I warn you, if you do not like the Comte and his methods, you will like mine even less, for I will have your brother arrested should you cross me."

She turns and walks away. I pause, imagining guards coming for Algernon and dragging him off. And yet, I know he would not want me to sit here passively, either. He would tell me that prison is the risk we must take if things are to change in this country.

And so I march back toward my room, feeling determined. For Mama and Papa and Jacques, for Algernon and Nicholas, for all of the people of France, it is time for some action. It is time to make the king realize that two can play a game.

Chapter Nine

I sneak out of my room late that night. Candles flicker eerily in the corridors, sending shadows bouncing about on the walls. Though the hour is late, servants still scurry about, answering the late-night calls of the royals or their guests. I know no one will question why I am up; still, I cannot be caught carrying out my plan. Earlier, I had felt the thrill of doing something dangerous. I could picture Algernon and his delight at my idea. I could see his white teeth gleaming with laughter and his eyes dancing with delight. Now my head pounds with the fear of being caught, alone.

I creep up the stairs to the very top of the Petit Trianon. I will methodically make my way through the palace floor by floor. Quietly, I tiptoe down the corridors, stopping by each door and examining it carefully. When a servant approaches, I draw back into the shadows, hoping I have not been spotted.

At last, I find what I have been looking for: a door that has a lock that is different from the traditional ones on the doors of the palace, a lock that is of the king's making. I take out the hairpins I have brought along and get to work.

As before, it takes several tries. This lock is completely different from the one Jean-Louis asked me to undo. I have to admit that the king is actually an excellent locksmith.

Slowly, I work my way through the palace, corridor by corridor, floor by floor, until at last, I fall into bed exhausted and triumphant. Altogether, I have unlocked over twenty doors. I smile to myself as I fall asleep.

☙

Madame Élisabeth is visibly upset when Manon and I arrive the next afternoon. She is on her knees praying when we enter her rooms, and she rises with a decidedly unhappy face.

"Last night, someone undid all the locks my brother installed in this palace," she says. "He is beside himself, demanding to know who has done this."

Manon shoots me a look. I keep my face neutral and calm, but inside, I am grinning with joy. The king is upset. Perhaps he will give up spending time making locks, now that he has seen that they are not impenetrable, and turn his attentions to the needs of his people.

"He is so distraught that he insists on my attendance at the public dinner tonight," Madame Élisabeth continues. "I have begged him to excuse me, but he is adamant. You know how he hates that display. And I hate it even more."

I have never seen the dinner, but I know that once a week, the king and queen have their meal outside where the public can come and view them eating. I am interested to see this spectacle, for I cannot imagine what it must feel like to watch your sovereign stuffing himself while your own stomach growls with hunger. I have a sudden memory of Maman's distended belly as she gave Jacques and me the last of our food, forgoing eating herself. Starvation is not a pretty thing to witness.

Manon slowly lays out the brushes and pencils for our lesson that day. "I understand, *madame*. But one meal is not so bad. The people who come to watch enjoy the experience very much. You are giving them a great deal of pleasure."

Madame Élisabeth sighs. "Why would someone enjoy seeing us eat?"

"For the same reason people pay to see you in wax at Manon's museum," I say, and then bite my tongue. I have spoken without being spoken to first—breaking a rule of the thick etiquette book.

But Madame Élisabeth laughs at my transgression. "Perhaps you could make a display of us eating for your museum, and we will no longer be required to put on these dinners."

Manon pauses. "That is an excellent idea, *madame*. If we have your permission to be there, I will have Celie do a drawing today and send it off to Dr. Curtius."

Madame Élisabeth nods. "If it will keep me from performing this obligation again, you may attend with my blessing."

A servant enters the room and whispers into Madame Élisabeth's ear. Madame Élisabeth's face grows white, and she rises quickly. "I am sorry, Manon, but we will have to forgo today's lesson. I must deal with another matter."

We curtsy deeply as Madame Élisabeth sweeps from the room.

I wonder why she is in such a hurry, what business would be so pressing that she would cancel our time together. Madame Élisabeth so rarely varies her routine that whatever it is, it must be important.

"I must write to l'Oncle about setting up this new exhibit," Manon says after the king's sister has gone. "You are free this afternoon, Celie, but you must be ready and dressed for this evening. A display of the king and queen eating dinner will bring in much money for us.

"And I have heard that your cohort in crime was delighted to get your drawing," Manon adds, her eyes on my face. "He asked if you could send another."

A delectable shiver passes through me at the thought of Algernon holding the picture I had in my hands just yesterday. It is as if he is in the room right next to me, and I bless the king's riders who are swift in delivering mail to Paris and back.

"Would that be all right?" I ask, trying not to sound too eager, although I am already considering what I can draw next that will bring a smile to Algernon's face.

Surprisingly, Manon nods her agreement. Her sudden willingness for me to send another drawing worries me. Why is she being so agreeable? My palms begin to sweat at the idea that perhaps she has discovered what we are up to, and is using Algernon and me. Perhaps she has made a pact with the king's men to help them track down Algernon, so they can arrest him while he is distributing Mirabeau's incendiary pamphlets.

I have no way to warn Algernon of this. I will simply have to hope that he is as wily as ever, and as cautious as he has been in the past.

"You may take the time this afternoon to do a sketch," Manon says. "And you may draw whatever you wish."

With these words, I grow more certain. Something is definitely not right. I will have to watch my step.

&

A short while later, I leave my room, on my way to the gardens. My mind is spinning, trying to decide how to draw something for Algernon that could warn him while still giving Mirabeau something he can use. Fear for Algernon makes me shiver. I know we must take some risks, but I still wish to bring about change with as little harm as possible to Algernon and myself.

So consumed am I by my dilemma that I do not notice the slightly open door until the sounds of crying from within make me pause. Jean-Louis is sitting on a chair, sobbing his eyes out. Is he in trouble again? Has the king installed new locks?

I am about to go to him, when there is movement from behind the half-shut door. Madame Élisabeth appears and kneels down next to Jean-Louis. "I am sorry, Jean-Louis. Your *papa* was so faithful to our family. I wish I could have saved him."

Jean-Louis's *papa* has died? A hard lump forms in my throat.

Jean-Louis wipes his tears and nods stiffly. "If your own physician could not help Papa, then there was nothing anyone could have done." Jean-Louis bites his lip, and I can see that he is trying not to cry again.

Madame Élisabeth puts her arms about Jean-Louis. "Come, cry all you want, child. You must not worry about being stoic for me. It is natural that you should cry."

"But Madame Élisabeth," Jean-Louis protests, "I am just a servant, and my tears may ruin your fine gown!"

"Oh, Jean-Louis," Madame Élisabeth replies, "we all live but a short while on this earth, royals and servants. None can escape this end. Just because I am of royal birth does not mean I cannot comfort a fellow traveler on this road we share.

"As for my dress," she adds, "if I should not hold a child who has lost his *papa* for fear of ruining my silk clothes, then I should not be fit to be thought human."

She holds out her arms. "Come, child. Come and let me hold you."

Jean-Louis goes to her then, and I hear him crying as if he will never stop.

Memories of my father roar back. I remember how soft his beard was when he kissed me at night. I remember his deep laugh when my mother sang off-key in our cottage. I remember the coldness of his hand in death. And I bite down hard on the inside of my lip to stop these memories, and to stem the tide of my own tears that I know will drown me if I ever let them come.

❧

That night, Manon brings me a new gown to wear for the dinner. It is a soft yellow silk decorated with a striped pattern in light blue threads, and silver buttons that shine in the candlelight. Manon hands me new stockings made of fine silk, and heeled shoes with highly polished buckles that sparkle with crystal stones.

"Jean-Louis's *papa* died today," I tell Manon.

I catch my breath as Manon pulls and tugs tight on the strings of my stays. But my mind is still on what I have seen. "Madame Élisabeth was with him. She sent her *personal* physician to take care of Jean-Louis's *papa*."

Manon's fingers stop pulling. "*Oui.* This seems to surprise you, Celie."

I think about Madame Élisabeth. I think of her servants and her dogs. I think of the lavishness of her apartments. Then I think of her praying, and of the wax figures she makes for the poor. I think of the way she did not scold me when I spoke out of turn, and how she had welcomed me and praised my gift for drawing.

"I have been with Madame Élisabeth for over ten years, since I was twenty years old," Manon continues, as she finishes tying the laces of my dress. "I have accompanied her on rides into the countryside, where she has given away much of her own allowance to help those in need. This past winter, we went out to distribute firewood and food to those who were hungry and cold. You see only the glitter and the waste, but there is much behind that façade."

I have to admit that Manon is right. Madame Élisabeth is a decent royal.

Manon pats me on the shoulder. "Come to me in half an hour. Let us go and see if we may help Madame Élisabeth end these tedious dinners she hates so."

I look at myself in the mirror, with my dress falling in lustrous folds about me. I realize then that if Algernon saw me now, he might take me for one of the privileged few, no different than anyone else who inhabits Versailles.

❧

Outside the palace, a horseshoe-shaped table has been set out, and lanterns have been placed strategically about the grounds to light the paths. The banquet table is wreathed in soft candlelight from two large candelabras that sit at each end. Already, crowds are gathering to see the royal family partake of their dinner. Guards patrol the grounds dressed in short robes, red pantaloons with a white swath on the side, and black shoes with buckles. Sashes tie their swords and halberds to their waists.

Madame Élisabeth has reserved us a place near the table. I immediately take out my paper, board, and pencil and get to work memorizing and sketching.

A moment later the musicians send up a chorus of sound, and the king and queen come out, dressed in purple ermine-lined robes. Madame Élisabeth follows, with two of her dogs. An excited murmur sweeps through the crowd, and people push up against me to get a better view of their sovereigns.

I watch the king and queen and Madame Élisabeth take their seats. They do not speak to one another, and the liveliness the queen had displayed at the Petit Hameau is gone from her face.

"He's a fat one, isn't he?" someone whispers.

"*Oui*, but our queen is lovely to look at," a second voice states.

I glance over my shoulder. Two people are standing behind me in clothes sporting holes and worn spots, their eyes sunken with weariness. They shiver as they stand there, the wind blowing through his thin coat and her threadbare shawl. But the man wears the required sword at his side, and the woman has on the mandatory stockings. They both beam at me with mouths missing teeth, as if they have just won a prize.

"Lucky to be here, aren't we?" the woman asks. "Isn't it thrilling to see our king and queen so close?"

I want to tell these people that this king they so revere spends his time putting locks on the doors of the palace rather than governing and that the queen likes to pretend she is a commoner for fun, while we are left to work the fields that provide the food now being served. But then I think about Madame Élisabeth's kindness. And so I say nothing.

I begin drawing again, sketching in the servant who stands behind the king and queen as he holds perfume burners that send out waves of sweet scent. Silver platters and china clink and clatter as plate after plate is delivered to the table. The smell of roast pheasant and freshly baked strawberry pastries wafts through the air. My stomach rumbles, and I wonder how the poor people behind me can stand there without fainting from hunger.

The royals do not speak. Occasionally, the king will put a small morsel into the queen's mouth himself before digging into his own plate piled high with delicacies, but the queen eats little else. Madame Élisabeth's face is blank, but I can see her feet tapping with impatience under the table.

The crowd stands in silence, too, staring at the royal family, as if they are some of the deformed characters that make up the shows in Paris. I continue to draw, but, as with the shows in Paris, I am uneasy about the whole spectacle.

At last, sweets are dispensed to the king and queen and Madame Élisabeth from a comfit box, and the dinner is over. The royal family rises and walks back into the palace.

"Are you done?" Manon asks.

I shake my head. "*Non*, but I have it all in my head. Can we walk into the gardens to a bench, and I will finish so you may send it to l'Oncle?"

"Come this way," Manon says, taking me by the arm when the path divides. "Most of the crowd will stay and stroll the gardens along the water, so let us wander a little further afield where you will not be disturbed."

I walk with Manon to a spot in the gardens that I have not yet been to. The smell of oranges drifts out in the soft night air from the greenhouses where they are grown. There I sit, my head bent, my mind whirling with the images I have seen tonight. I continue to draw while Manon rests beside me, looking out over the well-manicured garden in front of us. I am just about finished when I hear a sound that makes me jump. "What was that?"

Manon lets out a laugh. "I had forgotten. You have not seen the animals. Come. If you are finished, I will show you."

I rise and walk with Manon to a fence hidden behind tall hedges. Manon parts the greenery, and there before me are two of the strangest creatures I have ever seen, each housed in its own separate cage. "What are they?"

"One is called a lion, the other an ostrich. They come from the continent of Africa. The king ordered them brought here, for he is interested in animals of the exotic kind," Manon answers.

"Does he do anything with them?" I ask.

The lion lets out a roar again, and I shudder at the sound.

Manon shakes her head. "*Non.* They are just there to look at."

"They must be homesick," I say, looking at the caged animals. "It doesn't seem right to keep them locked up here so that people can just stare at them."

"Ah," Manon says, "it is not so different from tonight's dinner with our good king and queen then, is it, Celie?"

I open my mouth to protest, and then shut it just as quickly. Manon has a point. What difference is there between these caged animals being kept for the pleasure of the court, and the king and queen at dinner tonight being displayed for the pleasure of their people?

Do the king and queen feel like these animals that move about their confined spaces, restless with longing? Perhaps being born a royal isn't as easy as I imagine. The idea surprises me.

Then I shake myself. Life as a royal is certainly not as hard as the lives of those poor people tonight, shivering in the cold, tired from tilling their fields. Or as dangerous as Mirabeau's and Algernon's lives are now, slipping into the shadows of the alleyways of Paris to help these poor people end their misery, and hoping they are not caught and hanged in the process.

Chapter Ten

Not a week later, the heir to the throne, young Louis-Joseph, in his illness takes a turn for the worse. Doctors come and go, and all court entertainments are canceled. A hush settles in the hallways. Everyone walks about with serious faces.

And then, the unthinkable happens—the young prince dies.

I hear the news and immediately remember Jacques as my mother held him and he took his last breath. But Jacques had no one to stop his starving. It seems inconceivable to me that even with all their wealth and doctors and medicine, the king and queen could not save their little boy. And I realize that Madame Élisabeth was right. Even royals cannot escape death.

The court goes immediately into mourning, draping the halls with black, covering all their mirrors. Versailles becomes a prison of sadness. All signs of excesses and lavishness are banished. The courtiers are like deflated balloons. Everyone is gloomy and sad and worried.

The few glimpses I have of the king and the queen show two people who seem to have aged overnight. The queen is no longer the laughing, vibrant young woman I saw weeks earlier.

Their grief touches me, and I am surprised by this. And yet, they are human and I realize that in loss, we are all the same. I wonder how the king's starving subjects feel. Are they also in mourning? Or is their anger against their king so strong that they will find no sympathy for his loss?

Madame Élisabeth slips into despondency, canceling her drawing lessons and spending much time praying. I think about the other son, the eight-year-old boy who now is next in line to be king. In spite of our present king's ineffectiveness at ruling, I pray that nothing will happen to him. The country is in a bad enough condition without having to worry about an eight-year-old becoming ruler.

On our way back to our rooms one evening during these weeks of grieving, Manon says she is not feeling well, and that she wants to lie down.

"Is there something bothering you?" I ask, for I have noticed her pacing all day.

Manon's eyes slip from mine. "It's nothing. I just don't feel right. I will get some sleep tonight, and I am sure I will be fine in the morning."

I worry that perhaps Manon has caught the same illness that has killed the young prince. A flutter of concern enters my mind. I look closely at her, but she avoids my scrutiny by turning her back on me and closing the door to her room firmly behind her.

I stand in the hallway, concerned. But then my eyes light on a new lock on one of the doors. I wonder how the king has found the time or energy to do this while dealing with his sorrow. It angers me that he would play with locks only weeks after his son's death. Is he that callous?

I sigh. Perhaps I will be the one to fall ill from lack of sleep. For surely the king deserves to have his work undone tonight.

At dinner, I see Jean-Louis sitting alone at the servants' table in the kitchen. It is the first time I have seen him since his father's death. His little head is bent, and he looks completely dejected. I spoon out some bouillabaisse, then go to sit next to him on the bench.

"I heard about your *papa*, Jean-Louis," I whisper to him. "I am very sorry."

"At least I have not been let go from the palace," he says. His voice quivers.

"I heard that Madame Élisabeth made that possible," I say.

Jean-Louis keeps his head bent but nods.

One of the cooks sits down across from us and reaches over for the pitcher of wine.

"Like you, my *papa* and *maman* are dead, also," I tell Jean-Louis, my voice thick with memories, "and also my little brother."

"But now you have Mademoiselle Manon," Jean-Louis says.

I shake my head. "She is not family."

Jean-Louis looks puzzled. "But Mademoiselle Manon cares about you. I would be grateful to have someone who watched out for me as she does for you."

I cannot let Jean-Louis believe this, as it is untrue.

"Manon doesn't love me. She only brought me here to help her teach Madame Élisabeth how to draw. If my hands were useless, Mademoiselle Manon would not continue to feed and clothe me," I tell Jean-Louis.

The cook suddenly guffaws. "As if Manon could not do that herself."

I pause as I lift a spoonful of the fish stew to my mouth. "What do you mean by that?"

The cook shrugs. "Manon can draw well enough to train Madame Élisabeth. The king's sister has employed Mademoiselle Manon for over ten years now, and she has never been unhappy with her. Manon is thought of very highly by *all* the royals."

"But my drawings are superior to Manon's," I argue.

The cook takes a bite of bread and continues to talk with his mouth full. "I suppose they are, and it certainly helps Manon's museum displays to have you draw what you have seen. But Madame Élisabeth has no great need to draw as you do. Manon's abilities would have been sufficient."

"I was also brought here because Manon made a bet with the Comte d'Artois that she can control me. She has used me for that," I tell him.

The cook rolls his eyes. "Everyone knows about that bet, and Manon knows that she will never collect *anything*. She has always known that. The Comte's gambling debts are too great. He can pay no one, for there is no money in the royal coffers."

"What do you mean?" I say. "The royals have all this wealth."

The cook burps. "It's a façade. They live on credit, putting off one person they owe money to while honoring an older debt. And some debts they never settle. The Comte makes bets hoping he will win. But he never pays when he loses."

"Then why did Manon make the bet in the first place?" I ask in bewilderment.

"So you would help her with the museum," Jean-Louis says. He pauses. "And to save your life."

"That's impossible," I say, confusion snaking its way into my brain like smoke curls up a chimney. "She could care less about me."

Jean-Louis rises with his now empty bowl and spoon. "Then why are you not in prison, Celie?" He turns to walk away, stopping once to look back at me. "You aren't very smart, are you?"

The cook lets out a gruff chuckle.

And Jean-Louis leaves me, for the first time in my life, completely speechless.

∽

Late that night, I wind my way through the palace, candles flickering in their sconces, shadows bouncing off the walls of the hallways. I am uneasy. Since my talk with Jean-Louis, I have felt this shaky unsureness, as if I am making my way in a darkened room that I thought I knew well, only to find that someone has rearranged all the furniture.

Is it possible that Manon cares for me? Truly cares? That she sees me as more than a means to get her exhibits correct? I have to admit that I like her and l'Oncle and the aunts. The idea that Manon might have come to care for me, too, sends a strange surge of happiness through me and makes me less enthusiastic for what I am doing right now.

I hate this feeling of confusion. So I shake it off, and hurry on to do what I had originally planned.

The palace is strangely silent. Few servants roam, as if the entire palace is wrapped in a deep slumber. I hurry from lock to lock, but the workings of these new ones take longer than those I have opened before. The king has done well. His locks are frustratingly good. I blow a piece of hair from my eyes as I bend over each handle, my hands unsteady and my mind unsettled.

Slowly, the locks come undone. I unlock room after room, pushing each door open as quietly as possible as soon as the lock clicks its last pin. Four doors, five doors, six. As I open the seventh, suddenly a hand reaches out from behind the door and grabs firmly onto my wrist.

I am caught.

∽

Someone strong throws me across the room. I land heavily on the floor, hitting my head. Pain shoots through my temples. Black spots flood my vision.

"I knew it was you!" A man laughs.

Though the figure swims a bit before my eyes, my heart drops when I see who has caught me—the Comte d'Artois!

He walks by me, and calmly sweeping aside his coattails, takes a seat on a nearby chair, a smile on his face.

I think about making a run for it, but my vision is still blurry. I feel as if I might throw up at any moment. And that, I know, would only make matters worse, remembering how outraged the Comte had been about mud in his carriage. How will he deal with vomit on the floor?

"This is a *very* interesting situation," the Comte says. His voice is soft and low. He taps his long bejeweled fingers on his chin. "As I see it, there are two solutions to the situation facing us here, wouldn't you agree?"

I can only think of one—that he is going tell Manon what I have done. Manon will lose the bet. If, however, the cook has been telling the truth, perhaps Manon has always known she was not to win the thousand *livres*. It hardly matters. Either way, Manon will be angry, that much I am sure of.

I rise unsteadily to my feet. "Fine. Let's get it over with, then." The Comte chuckles. "Get what over with? Telling the king?"

My legs suddenly wobble beneath me. Tell the king? I had not even thought of that. What will happen to me then? Madame Élisabeth has said that the king is distraught over someone opening his locks. If the Comte reveals that I have done it, I will surely hang. And hanging had been not been a pleasant idea when I was living in the alley by the Palais-Royal. It is even less appealing now that I am doing a job I love, have a decent place to sleep, and have food in my belly.

I take a deep breath, push aside my panic, and turn to face the Comte. "That hardly seems necessary," I say. "Manon will be angry enough, I'm sure."

The Comte throws back his head and lets out a laugh. "Of that you are right, for if I tell the king that she has brought a thief to his court, she will lose her job."

Fear snakes its way through me with his words.

The Comte pauses. "Though not her life . . . as you will." He begins to pace about the room. "*Non.* Telling Manon is not the punishment I envision for you."

He turns to face me. "But perhaps it is not necessary to tell the king, either."

I look warily at the Comte, feeling like the animals caged in the king's menagerie. What is he planning?

The Comte sighs. "Ah, little urchin, you do not seem interested in my idea. I guess I shall just have to wake the king."

"I'm interested," I snap. "I just don't think I'll like it if *you* are suggesting it."

The Comte laughs.

"What are you offering?" I ask.

"The use of your skills for my silence," the Comte says.

"My drawing skills?" I ask, hope rising within me. Could it be that simple? "Do you want me to do a picture of you and your family?"

The Comte smiles and shakes his head. "I think not, although I have heard your abilities in that area highly praised. *Non*, Mademoiselle Celie. I was thinking more along the lines of your talent at cheating your fellow man."

The hairs on the back of my neck rise.

"As nothing is secret in this haven of intrigue where we live," the Comte says, walking about the room, "I am sure you are aware that I have a few gambling debts. I should like to rid myself of them."

"And you want me to help," I finish.

The Comte smiles again. "You may be a thief, but you are not dimwitted."

"Fine," I snap. "If it will keep you quiet, I will help you, although I don't see how you plan on having me attend your card parties. From what I have heard, they take place at the main palace, and Manon doesn't like me wandering off too far."

The Comte lets out another loud laugh. "Unless she is unawares . . . as it seems she is at present."

I scowl. "But you won't be playing cards at this time of night, now, will you?"

The Comte nods. "This is true. However, I shall tell Mademoiselle Manon that I need to observe you more closely. I will insist on your presence in the evenings, seeing as you are busy attending my sister during the day."

"You have this all figured out, don't you?" I ask.

"Ever since I heard about the locks being undone about the palace," the Comte replies. "So sit, little urchin. We have much to do to prepare for the next card game. We'll need to devise a system for you to relay to me my opponent's hand. You obviously can't be a blind beggar girl, so let us put our heads together and come up with a plan that will work."

I have no choice. Even if I were willing to face the king in order to avoid helping the Comte, I cannot risk Manon losing her job. The woman has been kind to me, and does not deserve to fall from favor because I have been foolish enough to think I could outwit royalty. And, too, there is just the sliver of hope in me that Jean-Louis is right, and Manon truly does care about me.

So I sit down on a chair beside the Comte, and spend an hour devising a way to help him cheat his friends.

❧

The Great Hall shimmers with the light of a thousand candles that reflect in the mirrors, as well as the silks and jewels of the ladies and men who laugh and talk, gamble and flirt. The smell of roast duck, fresh bread, and asparagus wafts through the room. Servants thread their way through the crowd, pouring wine, moving chairs, and delivering trays of sweetmeats, chocolates, and pastries.

In one corner, a group of musicians plays waltzes, and some men and women, depending on their rowdiness and inebriation, romp about and have a go at this new dance.

Round tables are set up all around the room, each containing courtiers gambling at cards or dice. Dogs lie at the feet of their masters as their owners smile at their winnings or frown at their losses.

I pause at the entrance to all this glamour and glitter. I have dressed as inconspicuously as I can. Still, I feel as noticeable as if I wear nothing at all. Never have I seen such an elaborate party. To think this happens every night horrifies me—the money it must cost, the lavishness and waste, are unconscionable.

In my hand, I carry a piece of paper, my board, and charcoal pencils. The Comte has managed to convince Manon to send me to him, but only by agreeing that I am to spend the evening drawing events in the Great Hall of Mirrors. Manon looked at me with such suspicion that sweat broke out on my brow.

The Comte and I have agreed that he will not acknowledge me when I enter the room. Still, I notice him glance my way as I delay at the doorway. So I pluck up my courage, take a deep breath, and enter the fray. I push my way through the crowds of people, being careful not to meet anyone's eye. When I get close to the Comte's table, I find a seat behind his opponent and settle down, my skirts tucked neatly around me.

A servant appears immediately at my side. "Would *mademoiselle* like some warm chocolate to drink?"

I instantly remember my first sip of that lovely brown liquid.

"Oh, *oui*," I respond without thinking.

I see the Comte frown and realize how silly I have been. How can I tap with a pencil if I have a chocolate in my hand?

"I mean *non, merci*," I say before the servant can leave. I nod toward my board. "I am here to draw."

He bows and walks away to serve the next person who seems empty-handed.

I roll out my paper and place it on my board. The noise level around me is deafening, with people laughing and talking and the musicians playing, and I feel a sudden stab of loneliness. How I wish Algernon were with me now! I can almost hear him grumbling over this display of wealth. If Algernon were here, he would have come up with a solution to my dilemma.

But I am alone with this problem, and for now there is nothing to do but play along with the Comte. And so I begin to draw, but slowly. I cannot get so caught up in my work that I do not pay attention to the Comte's opponent's cards. Yet the idea that I am actually helping the Comte makes me sick with loathing.

With my head lowered over my paper, I sneak a quick look at the Comte's table. The Comte's eyes are gleaming with pleasure.

His opponent takes a drink, letting his cards sway toward me. I see them and immediately begin to tap on my board, trying to look as if I am in deep concentration and stuck on a problem with my work. I have to tap loudly to be heard above the other noises, but no one seems to pay me any notice.

When I have finished, I begin to draw again.

"Ah ha, my win!" the Comte exclaims loudly, slapping his cards on the table.

"The night is early yet, my friend," his unsuspecting adversary says. "I wouldn't count on relieving your debt to me on one hand alone."

The Comte lets out a loud laugh. "Ah, dear cousin, I feel my luck is about to change for good."

"You are incorrigible," the Comte's cousin says, shaking his head and laughing. "But go on. Deal the next hand, and let us see if you can sustain this tiny winning streak of yours."

The Comte's cousin raises his finger, and a servant hurries over to him.

"*Oui*, Monsieur le Duc?" he asks, bowing low.

"More wine, please," the Comte's cousin commands.

The servant scurries off.

Two ladies come and sit beside me. They glance at me a moment, then seem to dismiss me as no one of importance and begin to talk between themselves.

"There are protests every day now in Paris," the one woman says. "My husband is afraid and wants us to leave France for my parents' home in Austria."

"What is the king to do?" the other woman says. "The commoners want a say in the government. Impossible! Can you imagine such a thing?"

"Those savages in America have put ideas into the people's heads," the other lady says. "And the king is too weak to squash these radical ideas. Until he stands up to these troublemakers, I fear we will be hearing of more unrest in the city."

I pause in my drawing. Can what they are saying be true? Are there protests in Paris? Has the time for the people's rebellion arrived? I will have to send Algernon another drawing quickly to help Mirabeau fuel the flames. I wonder why I have heard nothing of it in the servants' quarters?

A cough brings me out of my reverie. I have forgotten the card game. I bend over so that I can see the Duc's cards. When I straighten up, I find the two women looking at me oddly. Nervously, I make myself smile at them.

"A stitch in my side," I say. "I have been working so long at my drawing."

The women give me a nod, then go back to their conversation.

Quickly, I begin to tap out the cards before the Comte has to place his bet. When I finish, I go back to my drawing, hoping this will stop the women from noticing me at all. And soon, they are deep in conversation once again.

"The king takes no notice of anything that is happening around him," one of the women complains. "Look at him, sitting there, staring off into space. He hates these parties and doesn't mind showing it. Really, so inconsiderate of him."

I follow the woman's gaze and see the king, sitting alone and looking decidedly unhappy. I think back to the animals in his menagerie. How similar they look at this moment. Perhaps the king does not enjoy these spectacles at all. The idea that this might be true startles me.

"He was in a very jolly mood this morning," the other woman says, sniffing a bit. "It seems someone has discovered a way to undo those blasted locks of his."

I pause in my drawing, my attention now turned totally to the conversation of the two women beside me.

"He was like a child," the woman continues, "delighted that at last he has a worthy adversary with whom he can spar by creating better and tighter locks."

"Perhaps he could create a lock strong enough to muzzle the rabble of Paris," her partner comments, and the two women laugh.

I hear the Comte cough again and realize he has probably been trying to get my attention for quite some time. I ignore him and lean toward the two women. "Are you saying that the king was *happy* someone has unlocked his creations?"

The woman beside me pulls back, as if she has smelled something nasty. "It is inappropriate to eavesdrop."

"Please," I beg. "The king was truly *happy* about this?"

Beside me, the Comte bangs his drink down loudly on the table.

"Come now, cousin," the Duc says. "Place your bet. Or are you running a bit scared? Not a good hand, I suppose." The Duc chuckles.

"Please," I say again.

"*Mais oui*, he was happy," the woman snaps. "It is a game to him, one he has *always* enjoyed. Creating locks soothes him, he says."

"It's the *only* thing he seems to enjoy or spend time on," sniffs the other woman.

The Comte is coughing again and calling for water in a very angry voice.

Slowly, I rise from my place near his table. I turn and fix my eyes on the Comte. Then I walk to his table, pick up the Duc's drink, and throw the contents in the Comte's face.

I bang the empty glass down on the table and turn to the Duc, who is staring up at me with wide, startled eyes.

"He cheats," I say loudly, and without waiting to see what will happen, I walk from the room.

Chapter Eleven

I run to my room at the Petit Trianon, proud of having embarrassed the Comte, not bothering to stay and see what effect my words had on the Duc, and knowing the Comte will be furious. I am pleased to have let my anger finally roar out of me.

But as soon as the thrill of letting go has abated, I see the folly of my actions. Manon will be fired. And I will certainly be arrested. Now my stomach aches with fear, and there is nothing to do but ready myself for the guards to arrive.

I walk back and forth in my room, waiting, cursing myself for not controlling myself better, for not using my head. What have I done? What have I accomplished with my bravado?

But the Comte does not come, and this makes me worry more. Several times during the night, I hear noises outside my door. The blood pounds in my ears as I wait for the door to slam open, and the Comte's men to enter with their swords.

But in the end, it is not the guards who come for me. It is Manon.

"Get dressed," she commands, "and gather together all your things."

"Manon, I—" I manage to squeak out.

"Shush," Manon interrupts in a whisper. "Just do as I say, and do it quickly. Bring your suitcase to me when you are finished."

Manon walks out of my room without another word.

I rise and begin to pack. The room is already warm with summer heat, and my hands shake as I throw my few dresses into my suitcase. If the king forces Manon to leave, I cannot bear it.

At last, I finish. I drag my suitcase as quietly as I can across the hallway to Manon's room and knock softly. Manon opens the door.

She, too, is packed, her suitcase sitting on the floor of her room, her cupboard empty of clothes. I am mortified to have brought dismissal down on us both.

"Manon, I'm so sorry . . . ." I begin, my voice shaking.

Manon motions for me to be quiet. She goes to the window, pulls back the curtains, and looks out into the courtyard below.

"What is it?" I ask, wondering why Manon is acting so strangely, why she does not rant and rave and simply yell at me for my foolish act.

"Quiet, Celie!" Manon snaps. "I need to think."

I stand there, confused and uncertain.

There is a knock on the door, and a servant stands outside.

"Your carriage is ready, *mademoiselle*." He bows and then comes in to collect our bags. Behind him stands Jean-Louis. He looks at me with wide, frightened eyes.

Manon pauses on the threshold and looks about her. Abruptly, she turns toward the servant. "Hold the carriage for me. I won't be long."

"There are others waiting, *mademoiselle*," the servant begins.

"Jean-Louis, go and hold the carriage for us," Manon instructs, ignoring the servant. "Do not leave it, or give it to anyone else. Do you understand?"

"*Oui, mademoiselle*," Jean-Louis says, and he runs quickly from the room.

"Load our bags into that carriage," Manon commands the servant. "Come along, Celie, but keep quiet."

I realize then that whatever is wrong, it is something that does not involve Manon and me alone.

Dutifully, I follow Manon down the back winding staircase to Madame Élisabeth's rooms, curiosity making me forget my folly of that evening. What is happening? Why is Manon going to Madame Élisabeth at this hour? Manon scratches lightly upon the door, but it takes several minutes before an usher answers.

"*Madame* is praying," the usher says.

"I must speak with her," Manon says. "Now."

The usher looks insulted, but obeys Manon. For once, my mouth seems sewn shut with a thread that is strong and tight.

When Madame Élisabeth comes to the door, I see that she is fully dressed, though it is hours before dawn.

"Manon, my friend," Madame Élisabeth whispers, "you are leaving?"

"You are aware of what is happening?" Manon asks.

Madame Élisabeth nods. "*Oui*, I have been up and praying for hours."

"But I had heard that the court was unaware," Manon says.

Madame Élisabeth laughs lightly. "In this den of spies, do you think that I am not informed when there are public protests everywhere in the streets of Paris?"

My breath leaves me. So it is true. At last!

"Come with us then, *madame*," Manon urges. "You may stay at my uncle's house. He has bid me to return, but he has not said that I may not bring others. You could be in danger if this thing turns ugly. Please let me take you from here."

Why would it turn ugly, I wonder?

"I cannot leave my brother, Manon," Madame Élisabeth says gently. "But if your uncle has bid you return, go with my blessing. And when this issue is at last resolved, return to me, and we shall take up where we have left off."

"I cannot convince you otherwise?" Manon asks.

Madame Élisabeth gives a small smile and shakes her head. She turns to me and takes my hand. "It has been an honor to work with you, Celie. I hope to see you again very soon."

I nod, and then Madame Élisabeth shuts the door on us. I look over at Manon to see what we should do next, and to my amazement, there are tears on her cheeks. Whatever is Manon crying about?

೧

There is an even bigger surprise in store for me when we reach the kitchen and its door to the courtyard. Servants run hither and thither, clothing in their arms, bags being dragged behind them. They are arguing with one another and shoving one another. All seems to be in a state of confusion.

"Come, Celie," Manon orders, pushing her way through the crowd.

Outside, it is even more chaotic than in the kitchens. Darkness still hangs heavy in the sky, but the courtyard bristles with servants loading up bags and parcels and baskets of food.

"Manon," I finally ask, "what is happening?"

"You heard what I told Madame Élisabeth," Manon says. "There are public protests in the streets of Paris."

"But that is Paris, not here. And they are only protests," I say.

Manon does not answer me. Instead, she pushes me on ahead of her until she finds the carriage that Jean-Louis is holding for us.

"*Merci*, Jean-Louis," Manon says.

Jean-Louis bows low to us, but I can see fear in his eyes.

I cannot understand what everyone is so frightened about, but I look at the chaos surrounding us and do not want to leave Jean-Louis here on his own in all this bedlam. He can come with us now, and we can bring him back when the king has settled his differences with the people of Paris.

"We must take Jean-Louis with us," I say to Manon.

Manon halts her climb into the carriage. She turns to face me. "We dare not go back to ask Madame Élisabeth's permission to take him. We have tarried too long as it is."

"I'll be all right, Celie," Jean-Louis pipes up, but his voice cracks. "Don't worry about me."

I cannot look at his face and leave him behind. I have lost my little brother. I cannot leave Jean-Louis here alone to fend for himself.

"I'm staying with Jean-Louis," I announce.

"No, you're not," Manon says. "Get in this carriage now, Celie."

"*Non*," I say, folding my arms across my chest.

"Celie," Manon says, "I am your employer. Get in this carriage at once."

"Not without Jean-Louis," I say.

Suddenly, someone shouts. "There's a carriage that's not left yet. Grab it!"

"Celie, get in this carriage now, or we will have to fight people off to get out of here." Manon's voice is high and shrill.

"*Non*. Go on ahead if you wish. I will not leave Jean-Louis behind," I persist.

Without another word, Manon climbs down from the carriage. She reaches out an arm and grabs Jean-Louis, picking him up and shoving him into the carriage.

"Get in, Celie," Manon shouts. "Now!"

With Jean-Louis safely inside, I do not need to be asked twice. Several servants are running toward our carriage, bags in hand, angry looks on their faces. I scurry up the steps. Manon slams the door shut and raps on the carriage roof.

"To Paris," she yells.

The carriage rolls away, just as the servants who had intended to abscond with it reach us. It picks up speed until it is careening out the gates of Versailles, rocking back and forth on the road to the city.

Manon leans back against the cushions of the carriage, her face white. "If you ever do something like that again . . . ."

"I didn't want him to be there all alone," I say, defending myself.

Manon glances over at Jean-Louis, and after a moment, she sighs. "Perhaps you are right. There, he would have had no one to look after him."

"I don't understand. Why is everyone running about and trying to leave the palace, anyway?" I ask. "The people in Paris just want the king to help them. If he does that, everything will be all right."

Manon shrugs. "Perhaps. There has been trouble brewing in Paris for some time now. L'Oncle's letters to me have indicated that it is serious. He has had to make many changes, which is why he has been so accommodating with dresses for us and drawings for your brother. I don't know all the facts, but l'Oncle sent me a message during the night, telling me to get out as soon as possible. And when I went to the kitchen to gather some clothes I had left drying, the place was a madhouse. And I knew then that we had to hurry. Something is definitely astir."

I glance over at Jean-Louis. He hasn't said a word. He is just gazing out the carriage window as we speed along, but his brow is creased with uncertainty.

"Are you all right, Jean-Louis?" I ask.

"I am worried about the king and queen," Jean-Louis whispers. "Maybe I shouldn't have left. Some of the servants said the people would do away with them."

"That's nonsense," I tell him. "The people are starving, and they are angry. But the king is our king, and the people know that. It has been that way forever. There is no other way for it to be."

"Papa told me that in America they have no king or queen," Jean-Louis says. "He said that they rule themselves."

"But this is France," I say. "And we have always had a king. He just needs to pay attention to what is happening around him. He will talk to the people. It will be better for us all soon, right, Manon?"

"I don't know," Manon answers, her eyebrows knit with worry. "I don't know."

☙

The gates to the city are open and unguarded. I feel uneasy as we pass through them. What can have happened to make the guards leave their posts?

When we enter the city itself, we find the streets filled with the king's soldiers and groups of people huddled together, casting angry looks toward them. Everyone is wearing red, white, and blue rosettes pinned to their clothing.

"Why are they all wearing that?" I ask Manon.

Manon shakes her head. "I know as little as you do, Celie."

When we pull up at 20 Boulevard du Temple, my heart skips a beat. In a few minutes, I will see Algernon again. I have been gone but two months, and yet, it feels as if we have been parted for years.

L'Oncle opens the door himself when Manon knocks upon it. "Thank God. You and the child are safe."

He looks at Jean-Louis. "Who is this?"

"Another stray," Manon says shortly. "*Mon oncle*, what is happening? Is it true that the people are publicly protesting?"

"More like revolting," l'Oncle says. "They are determined to obtain gunpowder and guns. Soldiers have been called in to restore order."

"But why would they need guns and gunpowder?" I ask. "The people just want the king to listen. Mirabeau will speak for them."

L'Oncle snorts. "Child, this is a mob we are talking about, and mobs have a funny way of becoming something they were never intended to be—namely, violent."

For the first time, a shiver of fear runs through me over the thought of the people standing up to their king. I shake myself. What is wrong with me? I refuse to believe that something bad will happen. Only good can come from this.

"Where is Algernon?" I ask l'Oncle.

L'Oncle scowls. "Joined the rebels. However, I will say that he has also been keeping us safe because of his connections."

Safe from what, I wonder?

Just then, Manon's mother comes into the hallway.

"Maman, you are wearing those flowers, too?" Manon asks.

"It is a sign that you are a patriot. The colors red, white, and blue are meant to mimic the colors the Americans fly these days," Tante Anne-Marie says, setting down some firewood she has brought from outside and giving her daughter a hug. "You must never venture out without it, not unless you want to risk being harassed by the patriots. I am glad you are back and safe, Manon."

"We have had to change all the exhibits to keep from being badgered and shut down," l'Oncle tells Manon. "Our exhibits are no longer of the royal family, but of anyone who is considered a true patriot. I have renamed the museum. We are now the People's Museum."

"It has gone that far?" Manon asks.

"*Oui*," Tante Anne-Marie says. "I'm afraid so."

From outside, the sound of raised voices can suddenly be heard. Tante Marthe comes into the hallway. "There is a crowd coming this way, and it seems to be headed toward our doorstep." She gives Manon a quick hug and looks curiously at Jean-Louis.

"We will not answer," l'Oncle tells us. "Perhaps they will think us gone."

I cannot believe what they are doing. Why would they be so fearful of a little crowd, of people who just want to be heard?

There is a loud knocking on the door. "Open up. Open up now."

L'Oncle shakes his head and puts his finger to his lips. Jean-Louis moves closer to me and slips his hand into mine.

"Open up," the voice yells once again. "Open up in the name of the revolution."

Revolution? Why are they talking about revolution? Revolution is for the Americans, not us. We just want to be heard, not to overthrow our government or begin a revolution.

With these words, l'Oncle sighs. "It seems we *will* have to greet them."

Manon goes to the door. I peek around the side of Tante Anne-Marie, who has stepped in front of me as if I am in danger.

But I am determined to see exactly what is happening. The people of Paris are protesting at last, and I want to watch it happen.

Chapter Twelve

They carry torches in their hands, and are dressed in torn and ratty clothing. Their eyes shine with a light of excitement.

I come out from behind Tante Anne-Marie. These are my people, the people of the streets of Paris, the ones I have shared alleys with, the ones I have lost loved ones with, the ones who only want a roof over their heads and food in their bellies, the ones who want the king simply to listen to them and help them.

"We are marching for freedom today," one man says, stepping forward. "As head of the People's Museum, surely you will join us?"

"I'm afraid that's impossible," l'Oncle says. "We are currently in the midst of setting up a new display."

"But don't you want to support the cause?" a woman shouts.

The crowd presses closer. A voice here and there calls out, "Don't you?"

"Come now, *monsieur*," the man says, his voice low and menacing. "You wouldn't want us thinking you really aren't for the people?"

Just then the crowd separates, and there is Algernon. He is dressed in a uniform and looks more handsome than I can ever remember.

I am shocked to see him outfitted as a soldier. I know now how he must have felt seeing me dressed in lace and satins on the day I left for Versailles. He is no longer Algernon, boy of the streets. He is Algernon, a leader of the people of Paris. I stand frozen, for it is suddenly as if a stranger stands before me.

He gives me a mocking bow, his green eyes dancing. "No greeting for your brother, *ma soeur?*"

Slowly, I go to him. He reaches out and draws me close. His hands circle my waist, and I feel the warmth of his touch. My tongue is heavy, but I know I must say something to break the unnatural way I am feeling near him.

"Oh, Algernon, you are all right," I manage to say into the wool of his uniform.

"Did you miss me, Celie?" Algernon whispers, his breath hot on my ear. "For I have missed you."

I feel as if I will faint with his words.

I back away from him. "L'Oncle said you had gone to join the rebels."

Algernon gives me a wicked grin. "I am now a part of the people's new National Guard, which the National Assembly has established. I will help to maintain order as we face the king. The time of the people has come. It has come at last."

His handsome face glows. "Are you not happy, as we are, Celie?"

There are cheers from behind him.

"March with us, Celie, for I know you to be a true and loyal patriot, a supporter of the revolution," he urges.

Revolution. Why has Algernon, too, used that word?

"Oh *non*, Celie is staying right here," Manon says, suddenly stepping between us. "Those streets are no place for a young girl."

Algernon's eyes snap with anger. "She is no innocent, *mademoiselle*, not when it comes to knowing hunger or need. Or have you corrupted her so that she no longer understands what I have fought for, what we are all fighting for?"

Algernon swings his eyes to meet mine. "Have those fancy clothes you wear muddied your thoughts, Celie? Or are you still clearheaded enough to remember our time on the streets?"

I hesitate, looking from Manon, who perhaps cares about me, to Algernon, who has rescued me, and whom I love. What am I to do? I have waited years for this day, have suppressed the anger I have felt, have scrapped and stolen. Surely, Manon will understand this.

"I want to march," I say.

Algernon laughs with delight. "Ah, see how my sister has chosen me? Besides, dear lady, you cannot tell her *oui* or *non*. I am her brother, and I want her there. Come along then, Celie."

He holds out his hand, and I take it, feeling his fingers curl around mine, sure and strong. But I risk looking back once at Manon and am surprised to see that she is biting her lip, as if she is worried.

℘

We march through the streets of Paris, drums beating with our every step. Our footsteps ring loud on the cobblestones. As we march, more and more people join us until I can look back and see nothing but a sea of people, their faces burning with an inner fire. My spirits lift, and I join in the songs everyone has begun singing, patriotic songs, songs of freedom. Our voices rise as one into the smoky air of the city. Faces caked with grime and sweat, the common folk of Paris, smile at me. I join hands with Algernon on my left and a blacksmith on my other side.

I was right to come. This is where I belong, here with the people of Paris, here with those who cry for change, here with Algernon.

Down the Rue Saint-Martin and the Rue Greneta and the Rue Saint-Denis, we march, singing loudly, then onward down the Rue de la Ferronnerie and over to the Rue Saint-Honoré, until at last we reach the large square of the *Place Vendôme*, where we come to a sudden halt and the merriment ceases.

"Algernon, why have we stopped?" I ask, straining to see ahead.

"Soldiers of the king," Algernon tells me. "They are blocking our way."

"People of Paris!" A loud voice rings out across the sea of humanity. "Return to your homes. By order of your sovereign, the good King Louis the Sixteenth."

The crowd lets out shouts of derision. They boo the soldiers.

"We'll not turn back," someone yells.

"We march for freedom," someone else shouts.

The crowd cheers loudly.

"This is your last warning." The deep voice sounds again.

No one moves.

Suddenly, the sound of musket fire rings out.

Pandemonium ensues. People scatter, running everywhere, screaming. The crowd in front of me parts like a wave, and the soldiers are there, guns at their shoulders, bayonets pointed toward the fleeing crowds. On the ground, several people lie prone. One man is holding his stomach and crying as blood trickles through his fingers.

I am unable to move, shaken by the sudden violence and blood. What is happening? We have done nothing wrong. We have simply been marching, protesting the king's treatment of his subjects.

The soldiers begin advancing toward the remaining crowd, their guns at the ready. I stare in horror as a woman screams and falls, a soldier ripping his bayonet from her belly and running down an alley after the retreating protestors. I feel as if I will throw up. Will no one help these people?

I turn and see a soldier running at me, his bayonet aimed directly at my chest.

Before I can move, Algernon sweeps me up into his arms. He throws me over his shoulder. My head bounces crazily as Algernon runs down street after street, trying to escape the soldier who is in hot pursuit. But this time, there is no joy as we try to elude the law. This soldier is intent on killing.

"*Arrêtez! Arrêtez!*" the soldier calls after us.

I brace my hands on Algernon's back and look up. The soldier is getting closer. I can almost see his face.

"Hurry, Algernon," I shout.

A shot rings out, and I feel a slight breeze as the bullet passes in the air beside us.

Algernon whips us around a corner, and suddenly I am engulfed in darkness, swung in a half circle. And a door slams shut behind us.

Algernon sets me down and claps a hand over my mouth to silence me. But this time there is no tenderness in his touch. He is breathing hard, and sweat runs down his face.

My ears ring with the sound of shots and screams outside. The soldier who was chasing us pauses just outside our door. Algernon's eyes meet mine, and I feel as if even our hearts beating will alert the man outside to our presence.

But at last we hear him cough, and his footsteps move away.

"Why did they shoot at us, Algernon?" I whisper when the sounds of chaos finally fade and there is silence outside. "We were just marching. We weren't doing anything bad."

"They shot at us because they know we are right," Algernon says, his words broken up between the deep breaths he is now taking. "They are scared, for the time of the people has come, and the king is worried that his lavish lifestyle may be ending soon."

I have a sudden memory of the small, unhappy man who had been stared at by his own people as he ate, closeted in his own little world of Versailles. I want to tell Algernon that the king's world is hardly perfect, but now is not the time.

Looking exhausted, Algernon leans against the wall and slides down it until he is sitting on the floor in a heap. "*Merde!* We're lucky we escaped. Now we're stuck here until it grows dark, and I can sneak you back to Dr. Curtius's."

"You mean sneak us both back, don't you?" I ask, shuddering again at the thought of the violence I have just witnessed.

"*Non*, I have work to do," Algernon tells me, "important work. I will need to round up some patriots to keep peace in the city as these confrontations occur."

"There will be more?" I ask.

Algernon looks up at me as if I am daft. "Of course there will be more. This is what we have been waiting for, Celie."

I blink in surprise at his words. Is it? Is this what Algernon had envisioned when he spoke of rebellion? Hadn't he simply been talking about eliminating taxes and getting bread to the people? I know that is what I wanted.

Had he meant this? This violence and chaos?

Surely, this is an isolated incident in the path toward equality. Surely there will be no more violence, for what purpose does it serve? The king's men cannot kill all those who want freedom in France.

"We will all have to do our part," Algernon continues. "It would be wise for Dr. Curtius to join our National Guard, as I have."

"How can he?" I ask. "He has worked for the king."

"L'Oncle, as you call him, is a smart man," Algernon says. "He knows the winds of change when he feels them coming. You and the lady will not be going back to Versailles anytime soon."

The events of the day, the ride from Versailles, the march, the shooting, all combine to finally overwhelm me. I slide down the wall next to Algernon and lean my head against his shoulder. I can no longer think straight.

"Algernon," I ask, my voice sounding small and frightened even to me, "what will the *people* do now?"

Algernon shrugs. "Hopefully this incident will enrage them, make them stand up for their liberties," he responds.

"How?" I ask.

"By taking up arms."

"Against their own king?" I cry, sitting up.

"Against anyone who will not listen to their demands," Algernon snaps. "I think they will keep trying to make themselves heard, even if they have to march all the way to Versailles."

"Will there be fighting between them?" I ask.

Algernon looks at me with exasperation. "Did you lose your mind at Versailles, Celie? What did you expect? Our king has done nothing while his people wither away in poverty? Have you forgotten your *maman* and *papa*?"

Of course I have not forgotten, but I am confused. I had not thought that freedom for the people might mean death and killing. I had thought it meant talking to the king, getting him to see reason. I don't want to think about this anymore. I sit silent, and eventually, I feel Algernon's frustration with me has passed.

"Where are we?" I ask, looking around at the small room in which we are ensconced. There is a single bed against one wall, on which lies a tattered blanket and a chamber pot that is half full, with mold around its edges.

"It's one of many hiding spots used by the revolutionaries," Algernon says. "*Mon Dieu.* I was lucky to remember it just now. Otherwise, we'd be lying out in those streets bleeding to death, too."

My mind flits back again to the grand rooms of Versailles with their silk curtains and gilded oil paintings. I look once more around the sparse room and shiver.

"You're freezing," Algernon says.

I nod.

He goes to take off his coat and give it to me, but I lean in toward him instead. I feel him stiffen for a moment.

But at last, he relaxes and puts his arm about me and pulls me close. I fall against his chest and wish once again for Algernon to let the memory of Julia go.

But until he does, I will sit here and be soothed by his warmth. Within minutes, the rhythm of his beating heart lulls me to sleep.

∞

When I wake, I am in bed in the green room at l'Oncle's house. Vaguely, I remember Algernon carrying me back. It is dark outside, and I am relieved to be here, safe and sound. I shiver, remembering the awful violence at the Place Vendôme.

In the hallway, I hear whispering voices and someone saying my name.

I rise from the bed and tiptoe to the door. Who is talking about me?

"No, I cannot do it," I hear Manon say. "I cannot make them leave. And where would they go? Where would Celie go?"

My heart thumps at her words. Will l'Oncle and Manon turn us out? After all this time? And she is right. Where would we go? I think of our ride yesterday through the city and the angry looks of the people. I think of the march. The streets aren't as safe as they were when Algernon and I slept in the alley. Now, all seems to be confusion out there.

"I agree that having Algernon on our side helps with the National Assembly, but if the king should squash this rebellion, we could be in trouble for harboring them," l'Oncle whispers.

"The king will not forget all my years of service to his sister," Manon argues. "And Algernon can keep us out of harm's way, should the revolutionaries take over completely. We are safe either way. The only thing that matters is survival through this chaos, uncle."

L'Oncle gives a sigh. "Perhaps you are right."

Relief floods through me as I realize I have been holding my breath.

"Good. For I cannot turn her out," Manon says. "I know she is a thief, but she has a good heart. I have come to care for her as a daughter over these last weeks. And I think you have, too. Her art touches you, does it not?"

There is a long pause. "Oui, Manon. I, too, care for her."

"Bon," Manon says. "It is settled. Now, let me go check on her."

Swiftly, I fly to the bed and close my eyes. So it is true. Manon does care for me. I am astounded at how this knowledge warms me, makes this very bed suddenly feel like home.

I hear her footsteps near me, and I open my eyes to look upon the woman who thinks of me as a daughter.

"You're awake," she says.

"Today was awful, Manon," I tell her, as my fears and thoughts spill out in a torrent, let loose by her support of me.

She sits down upon the bed beside me and gently smoothes back the hair from my face. "I know. Word has spread about the city."

"I don't understand," I say, thinking back on our time together at Versailles. "Why would the king order the soldiers to shoot at his own people?"

"You've seen the king," Manon says. "Do you think *he* sent those orders?"

I shake my head. "Then why did they shoot?"

"Frightened people do foolish things," Manon says.

"But why were they frightened of us?" I ask, still bewildered. "We had no weapons."

"Words are weapons, Celie," Manon says, "as are symbols. Never forget that. The power of change can come not just by force, but by speech or a peaceful marching crowd."

I breathe in the lavender scent of the lady.

"Now go to sleep, *ma petite*," Manon says. "All will look better in the morning light."

I pray that she is right.

Chapter Thirteen

Jean-Louis jumps from his chair when I come down to breakfast. In the chaos of yesterday, I had forgotten him.

"Celie!" He throws his little arms about me.

"The boy barely slept a wink last night," Tante Anne-Marie says, smiling. "He went to your room over and over to be sure you were all right."

"Foolishness, if you ask me," Tante Marthe grumbles. "Why a man would ever take a young girl to a protest march is beyond me. I knew that scoundrel was no good, and I was right."

"Algernon didn't know it would turn violent," I protest, defending Algernon, even though I am no longer sure that this is entirely true.

"Then your *brother* has got rocks in his head," Tante Marthe spits out. "Now sit down and eat. Do you think I have all day to make breakfast?"

I sit down next to Jean-Louis, who scoots his chair closer to mine. It is good to be back in l'Oncle's house, back with the aunts and Manon, and to have Jean-Louis with me. It is an oasis from the violence I have just witnessed.

The door from the museum swings open, and Algernon comes in with l'Oncle.

Gratitude fills me once more that we are here, safe, and not out on the streets.

"I've just come to tell you that I'm off, Celie, but Manon and Dr. Curtius have agreed to watch over you until I get back," he says.

My smile disappears. "Where are you going?"

"To help out with the cause. We talked about this yesterday," Algernon says. "Don't look like you didn't expect it. How many times have I told you that I would be involved in the revolution if the moment ever came?"

"Rebellion," I protest, hating the word *révolution* and not wanting him to go, fear for his safety thick in my throat. "And I thought we would be together."

"You want to go with me *now?*" Algernon asks, looking me directly in the eye. "You want to sleep in alleyways or sewers if the king's men decide to root you out, scuttle about town with messages that could land you in prison or worse if you are caught?"

"*Non,*" I answer, "but I don't want you to do that, either. What if there is more violence? What if you get hurt?"

Algernon kneels beside me. He takes my hands in his. "Celie, I must do this. It is who I am, what I was made for. And I promise to come for you when it is time for you to join me."

I think of Julia. He is getting his revenge at last.

"What if I need you before that?" I manage to say.

Algernon's eyes soften. "If you should need me, tie a ribbon to your door. Our people will watch for it, and they will let me know."

He rises to go.

"Please just stay here, Algernon," I try, begging one last time.

"I can't, Celie," Algernon says, his voice soft but firm. "You know I can't."

I do, but it doesn't make me feel any better when I watch him walk out the door. And it is all I can do not to run after him.

જ

The day passes quietly enough, but the next morning, Jean-Louis comes running into the kitchen, sweat on his brow.

"Where is the water from the water man, Jean-Louis?" Tante Marthe asks, rolling her eyes. "Was the bucket too heavy for you to carry again? Celie, go help him, *s'il te plaît*."

"*Non. Non*," Jean-Louis cries. He stops to catch his breath.

"What is it?" Tante Anne-Marie says. "What is wrong, Jean-Louis?"

"They have . . . ." He coughs. "The people have descended on the *Bastille*."

"The old prison?" Manon asks. "Whatever for?"

Jean-Louis pauses, takes a deep breath. "They went to get gunpowder and muskets. They mean to fight against the king's soldiers."

"What?" I ask.

Jean-Louis looks at me. "There have been shots fired."

"Was anyone hurt?" I ask. I think of Algernon, and for a moment, I cannot breathe.

"I don't know," Jean-Louis says. "That is all I have heard."

Manon rises from her chair at the table. "Wait here. All of you."

She returns in a moment with l'Oncle. He wears a National Guard uniform, which startles me.

Algernon was right. L'Oncle has sensed the winds of change, and he has turned with them. In the space of a day, he has outwardly dropped his loyalty to the king. He is a revolutionary, as Algernon predicted he would become. He dons a hat and nods at us all. "I'll be back."

"Where is he going?" I ask.

"To see what is happening," Manon answers.

❦

An hour later, the sound of singing rings out loud and clear from the streets. Jean-Louis and I go to the window. Down the

Boulevard du Temple, thousands of people march, some carrying pitchforks, some carrying muskets.

A loud banging is heard in the front hall. The knocking is repeated, stronger and more insistent, as if thousands of fists are pounding on our door.

I follow Manon into the hallway. "Keep back," she orders Jean-Louis and me. "Both of you."

Tante Anne-Marie comes from the kitchen, wringing her hands. "Oh, if only l'Oncle were here."

"Well, he isn't. So we shall have to deal with this on our own, Maman." Manon takes a deep breath and opens the door.

The crowd stands before us. A man is at the front, a large grin on his face, and in his hand, is the bloody head of the governor of the Bastille Prison.

"*Mon Dieu*," Tante Anne-Marie says, her hand going to her chest.

I bite back a scream. Have the king's soldiers beheaded their own governor?

"*Oui*, it is quite a sight, *n'est-ce pas?*" the man holding the head asks. "The first of many heads that shall be rolling, if the people have their way."

"The people have done this?" I cry before I can stop myself.

"*Oui*," a woman shouts out. "He wouldn't let us in to have our gunpowder."

"What would you want gunpowder for?" I ask.

"Shush, Celie," Manon snaps.

She turns to the crowd gathered at her door. "What do you want with us?"

"We want you to make one of those wax heads from this," the man says, holding the decapitated head higher, "and put it in your museum." Blood drips down his arm. Behind him, the crowd lets out a loud cheer.

"*Oui*, we wish to show the country what can happen if the king's soldiers oppose us again," someone else shouts.

"We make heads from drawings," Manon tells them, "not from real ones."

"Today you'll make a wax head the way *we* want you to make it," the man snaps.

"Very well," Manon says, her face impassive, as if she receives requests like this every day. "Celie, go make some plaster."

I feel as if my feet are nailed to the floor. Does Manon truly mean to do this? Beside me, Jean-Louis whimpers.

"Celie. Now." Manon's voice is sharp.

"Don't bark at the child," the man in front says, grinning and revealing several black teeth. "We'll just go with you into your museum, *n'est-ce pas?* That way, you needn't bring your things out into the street."

Manon blocks his way. "Sorry. But the museum is closed at the present."

How can they have done this? How can they have *murdered* someone? And how can they take such *pleasure* in it? Don't they understand that by murdering someone, they are no better than the king's men who fired at an innocent crowd only two days earlier?

I do not want these people in here any more than Manon does. These are not the people, the true people of France. These people are mad, violent, crazy.

I come to my senses, turn, and walk quickly to the back room, my mind racing. Where is Algernon? And where is l'Oncle? Why have they not prevented these nasty people from coming here? Why have Algernon and Mirabeau not stopped them from committing this awful act?

I grab the sack of plaster dust and mix it in a bucket of water. My hands shake, and I spill some dust on the floor. I take a deep breath to steady myself. I have to be sure that the consistency is right, yet I sense that if I do not hurry, the crowd will force itself into Manon's home like a rushing river overflowing its banks. At last the mixture is ready, and I head back with the plaster and brushes.

Calmly, Manon takes the plaster and the brushes from my hands, thanking me. "I will need your help," she says.

"My help?" I ask, my voice squeaking in shock.

"Maman, take Jean-Louis inside and close the door," Manon commands. "Celie and I will be in shortly."

Tante Anne-Marie does as Manon asks her.

"What do you want *me* to do?" I ask.

"I will need you to apply the plaster," Manon says.

My heart beats wildly in my chest. How can I work on a dead man?

"I will hold the head steady for you," Manon says. Then she lowers her voice. "Please, Celie. If we do not do this, I fear the crowd will have our heads also."

I had not thought of that. I nod, my stomach already queasy. Reluctantly, I follow Manon out into the street, the crowd parting as we walk through. I see in their faces that they are filled with excitement. It sickens me even more. Who are these people who welcome this violence?

Manon kneels in the dirt of the street. She turns to the man who holds the governor's head. "Please hand him to me."

The man laughs and tosses the head to Manon. Like an overripe melon, the head makes a squishing sound as Manon catches it, which almost makes me throw up.

Manon does not blink. "Come along, Celie. Let us begin."

I kneel down. My hands tremble as I take up the brush.

Manon turns the head until the dead man's eyes stare up at me, unseeing. I look at him, and Papa's lifeless eyes waver in front of me. I gag.

"Steady," Manon says in a low voice.

I swallow the sickness in my throat. With shaking hands, I dip the brush into the wet plaster and then begin slowly applying it to the dead governor's head.

"Oooh, don't he look good, all covered in goo?" someone yells out.

The crowd lets out a cheer.

"Keep your brush strokes even, Celie," Manon says.

I look up and find Manon looking fixedly at me. I lower my head and go back to work, keeping my mind on Manon's calming voice as Manon softly speaks, instructing me the whole way, as if I have never cast a plaster mold before.

When we are finished with the face, Manon sits back on her heels. "We must let it dry for a bit," she informs the crowd, looking up at them. "You could go on, and I will finish the job."

"*Non, merci*," the man who has been at the front of the crowd says. "We will wait until you are done."

"*Oui*," the crowd calls out in agreement.

"We want all of France to see his head," someone else yells.

Manon looks over at me. "Then we shall finish as fast as we can."

The crowd mills about as the plaster dries, and finally, Manon removes the cast from the governor's face. Next, we do the sides. This is easier for me, as the poor man's dead eyes are not gazing up at me as I paint. And if I do not think too much on it, I can almost imagine the ear I cover is but a clay mold.

At last, the four sides of the head have dried and are removed. Manon hands the head, which is beginning to smell of rot and cave in on itself, back to the crowd. "You shall see your villain in the museum in a few days."

There is a roar of approval, and the crowd turns and begins to march away, the unfortunate governor's head stuck on a pike and held at the front of the line.

When they are gone, I can contain myself no longer. I collapse, horror finally overwhelming me. Tante Marthe comes out from inside the house and picks up the four molded plaster casts of the governor's head.

Manon reaches down and helps me to my feet. "It is over, Celie."

"I want a bath," I whisper. "I smell like that dead man."

When the water is hot, I climb into the tub. I grab the soap from Tante Anne-Marie and begin to scrub as hard as I can. Yet try as I might, I cannot get the smell to leave me. I cannot get the sight of the dead man to vanish from my eyes.

How has this happened? How could the people kill someone and laugh about it when they have witnessed these very same things done to them? What terrible evil has been unleashed? All my lovely dreams of equality are being shattered, one violent act at a time.

At last I feel a hand on my shoulder. I look up to find Manon, clean and in a dressing gown. "The water is cold, Celie. You must get out. I don't want you getting ill."

"I already feel ill," I say, but I do as Manon tells me.

Manon throws a warm nightgown over my head. Still, I shiver.

She pulls a chair toward the fire and settles me in it, wrapping a blanket firmly around me. Then she sits next to me.

"Why have they done this?" I ask, my voice sounding as hollow as if am speaking in the spaces under the bridges that cross the Seine.

Manon puts her arm around me. "When change comes to a country, it does not always come easily, Celie. Change is often accompanied by violence."

"They could have just tried talking to the king," I say. "He might have listened."

"*Oui*," Manon agrees, "he might have, or he might not have. He lives in a world so apart from the common people, it may have been impossible for him to understand the depths of his people's anger."

"Maybe he will understand now," I say, raising my eyes to Manon's. "Perhaps he will come to Paris and talk to them, and all will be well."

But Manon shakes her head. "I believe it is past that now, Celie. Revolution is upon us. And we must keep our heads low, and our loyalties to ourselves."

I think of where my own loyalties lie—with Algernon, with Maman and Papa and Jacques. I believe in them. I still believe in the idea of equality for everyone. But not like this. Never like this.

"And where do your loyalties lie?" I finally ask Manon.

She sighs. "I am loyal to us. I am for our survival."

She shakes her head. "But I believe that now we must draw deep into ourselves, Celie, for the courage and fortitude to survive, for I believe that there is worse to come."

Chapter Fourteen

A few weeks later, I wake, my eyes feeling as if they are three times their regular size from lack of sleep. Nightmares are my constant companions these days.

When I go downstairs and take a seat, Jean-Louis scoots his chair next to me, and lays his head on my shoulder. Since the day of the governor's beheading, he has rarely left my side.

L'Oncle comes into the kitchen as I am taking the last bite of my breakfast brioche. He pulls out a chair. "Jean-Louis, I believe Tante Marthe is calling for you."

"I don't hear anything," Jean-Louis says.

"Perhaps not," l'Oncle says. "But please go and find her."

Jean-Louis reluctantly slides from his seat and dawdles at the door.

"Jean-Louis," l'Oncle says, sternly. "Go. Now."

Slowly, Jean-Louis walks away.

L'Oncle turns to me. "I have been meaning to apologize to you, *ma petite*. I'm sorry that I was not here when they came with the governor's head. It was a terrible thing that you had to do."

"That's all right," I tell him, but my voice sounds wooden.

"As National Guardsmen, both Algernon and I were at the Bastille," l'Oncle says. "But there was such confusion at the prison that Algernon and I were kept quite busy restoring order, and we were unable to follow the crowd when they took off with the head of the dead governor. Things have been unsettled these past weeks, and I am sorry that it has taken so long for us to have this talk."

"Is Algernon all right?" I ask. I have not seen him since the incident at the Bastille. He has been kept from our home, running National Assembly errands.

"*Oui*, he will be here shortly," l'Oncle says. "But Celie, there is something we must discuss now."

He holds out his hand. In it is a paper pamphlet, and on the front is my drawing of the naval battle on the Grand Canal at Versailles. "I think perhaps that it would be wise for the artist of this picture to stop inciting the people with more drawings of the excesses of the court. They were inflamed enough with this particular one, which was given to me that day at the Bastille. I recognized your work immediately. But I think it would be best now if no more were to surface. Would you not agree, *ma petite?*"

Bile rises in my throat. Did my drawing and Mirabeau's reproduction of it cause the events at the prison? Can it be my fault that the headless body of the governor lies somewhere, beaten and unattended? I had wanted my drawings to prompt discussion, not incite violence. *Mon Dieu!* Am I responsible? Me, who hates violence with a passion?

"I did not mean for . . . I did not know that . . . ." I stammer.

"I know. I understand," l'Oncle says, placing a hand on my knee.

"*Mon oncle*, did my drawings cause that brutality?" I burst out, as shame and guilt wash over me at the possibility.

"*Non, non,*" l'Oncle says quickly. "Your drawings did not cause that uproar. Please do not think yourself at fault for what others chose to do. But Mirabeau's use of them has lit a spark. I would not want you to be the cause of any more of these types of incidents. Would you?"

If there is even the slightest chance that my drawings will incite fresh violence, I will rip my own drawings to shreds.

"It will not happen. I promise," I tell him, still shaken.

"*Bon,*" l'Oncle says, rising. "That is what I was hoping to hear."

Algernon comes into the kitchen then, and relief rushes through me as I see he is whole and unharmed.

But his face is flushed, and his eyes glow with an odd light.

"They are marching to Versailles."

"Who?" Manon asks, as she joins us along with Jean-Louis.

"Women, thousands of women," Algernon says, turning to include them. "A group of market fisherwomen began a protest, and thousands of other women joined them. Together, they are marching to Versailles. The women mean to bring the king to Paris so he can witness the poverty and hunger of his people."

"The king will never leave Versailles," Manon says.

"They are armed, Manon," Algernon says. "They have ropes and knives, and they are angry. I would not want to be the king when they meet him."

My breath quickens at his statement. Will there be more violence now?

"Will they hurt him?" Jean-Louis pipes up. "Would they hurt their king?"

Algernon shrugs. "Perhaps. And why shouldn't they? He has done nothing for them. There have been protests, and he has seen the pamphlets that accuse him of neglect. And still, he has done nothing."

Algernon looks hard at Jean-Louis. "He will get what he deserves."

Jean-Louis puts his head down, and I can see his shoulders shaking. He is crying. I know Algernon is aware that Versailles and the king are the only home Jean-Louis has ever really known, and I am angry with him for being so hardhearted with Jean-Louis.

"Come along, Celie," Algernon says. "I have brought a cart, and we will go together to see what these women are able to get from our almighty sovereign."

"You are not taking her out in those streets again," Manon says vehemently.

"This is history, Manon," Algernon says. "I want my sister there to see it."

"Let us be done with this charade. She is not your sister," l'Oncle snaps at Algernon.

Algernon and l'Oncle glare at one another, and I am left to choose sides again.

I have dreamed for years of a time when the king would listen to his people. I have longed for a day when families like mine might be treated more kindly, thanked and honored for their service to their country. And yet, this *révolution* is not how I had wanted to go about it. The violent anger that has erupted is like a wild animal that cannot be controlled. These events in the quest for equality have taken twists and turns that leave my head spinning and my heart weak.

"Come, Celie," Algernon says softly, moving near me and bending over to put his lips near my ear.

"We are wasting time," he whispers.

"I . . . I don't feel well," I stammer.

I need to think.

"That's a shame," Algernon says, pulling me up to stand with him. He places a hand around my waist, but for once, I wish he would not touch me. "Feeling ill on the most glorious of days, when all we have worked for, all Mirabeau has spoken for, all we have envisioned, is happening."

He bends near me and takes my chin in his hand, turning my face up to his. He looks curiously at me, and I wish I could sink into the ground rather than meet his inquiring gaze. Can he see how badly I do not want to go? Can he tell that I no longer want to be a part of this new madness, his companion in crime, his partner?

"I need you by my side, like before," Algernon says, his voice tender. "There is so much to do, so much to watch unfold. The next days are going to be busy ones for us and for the revolution. Mirabeau is the leader now, and we will go sliding in on his coattails, thanks to you and your drawings, and my willingness to be his right-hand man. We need sleep in the streets or here no longer. Our dreams are coming true."

I feel as if I will choke with the mention of my drawings. I can pretend with him no longer. "I don't want to go."

I finally look at him directly. "This isn't what I saw happening, Algernon. This isn't what I thought would occur. I am for rebellion, but not this. I don't like the way you are treating and speaking of the king."

Anger distorts his face.

"Did you think revolution could be obtained without some force?" Algernon says, his voice rising. "Did you think a king could be brought down without a struggle?"

"I believed people could be reasonable, Algernon," I say, my voice rising, too, as I see him slipping away.

"Then you are a fool!" Algernon snaps. "I should have known this might happen, sending you out to live in a palace like that. They have corrupted you. And now you are the king's girl, are you?"

"I am my own girl, Algernon," I say wearily. "I don't like violence. I never have."

"No one likes violence," he snaps. "But sometimes it is necessary."

"No," I argue, "it is never necessary. One can use words and wit, as we did."

Algernon laughs. "Yes, look how far our words and wit got us."

"It got us a home and a roof over our heads," I remind him.

"Have you completely forgotten your *maman* and your *papa*?" Algernon counters. "Have you forgotten how they died?"

"*Non*," I say. "But I will not do to others what was done to them. Otherwise, I am no better than they are."

I turn from him, for I cannot bear this leave-taking now that I have made my decision. "I'm done with this, Algernon. This violence isn't for me."

"I'll not be there, should you need me," Algernon says, his voice taut with anger. "Don't plan on coming to me, when Manon no longer has use for you and turns you out. I won't take you back."

I don't answer. I can't.

I run from him to my bedroom before I have time to change my mind.

Perhaps Algernon is right, and Manon will tire of me and throw me out. Perhaps I will end up back on the streets. I don't care. For I finally know the truth: I would rather die in the streets than see one more innocent person murdered. I will not walk down that alley ever again—not even for Algernon.

ه

The king and his family, including Madame Élisabeth, are forced by the fish women to come to Paris. For a while, the revolutionaries and the king try working together, but when the king and his family try to flee the country and are caught, all trust is lost.

The royal family is put in the Temple, a dark and decaying royal palace, now a jail. They become prisoners, their freedom revoked.

The National Assembly takes over running the country. It saddens me that the king has been rendered powerless, and I am infuriated when I learn that the Comte has escaped to Austria. But conflicting emotions seem to be my constant companions these days.

Algernon is true to his word. He does not come back, and I am bereft of the boy who rescued me. My heart aches every day for him.

People who own apartments near the Temple prison grounds start to offer Parisians a glimpse of their sovereigns for a price.

"Manon," Jean-Louis says, "I would like to go and see the king and queen."

"Did we not agree to stay away, Jean-Louis?" Manon reminds him.

"Please," Jean-Louis pleads. "Just once. I won't ask again."

"I'll take him," I offer, realizing that the king and queen were like family to this little boy, who has lost so much.

Manon hesitates, then relents. "Fine. Once. But I do not want you lingering there or trying to get their attention. It will only alert people to the fact that you know the royals. It's best we keep that to ourselves."

Jean-Louis's face lights up. "*Merci*, Manon."

That afternoon, Jean-Louis and I walk through the streets of Paris. Near the Temple prison, there are people calling out the cost of glimpsing the king and queen as they walk the grounds for some air.

Over the past few days, Tante Anne-Marie and Tante Marthe have listened carefully at the market and know which apartment has the best view and what time is optimal for seeing the royal family. I wonder if Algernon is enjoying this—making a spectacle of the king and his loved ones in this fashion.

I pay the two *sous* for Jean-Louis and myself. We climb five flights of rickety wooden stairs and are shown to a window with the sash open. Jean-Louis leans out.

"There they are," the owner says, pointing, "the queen and her children."

"That's not the queen," Jean-Louis says.

"And how would you know what the queen looks like?" the owner asks, his eyes narrowing suspiciously.

I pinch Jean-Louis. Why is he saying this?

"I don't," Jean-Louis squeaks. "But we had heard that she is beautiful."

"No longer," the owner of the apartment says. "Her hair has turned white, and she has wrinkles like the rest of us. But believe me, that is the same wicked, foreign queen who has taken bread from the mouths of our children to dress herself finely. Not so good-looking now, is she?"

I glance out the window and see in a moment why Jean-Louis has spoken. The woman with the royal children in the garden looks like an old woman, and yet, it is Marie Antoinette herself.

The man chuckles.

I grab Jean-Louis and pull him from the window. I do not want him to begin crying in front of this man. And I cannot bear to look anymore either.

∾

Several weeks later, I wake to screaming. I go into the hallway to find Jean-Louis standing there, looking as scared and bewildered as I am.

Together we go downstairs to find Tante Anne-Marie on her knees, keening and wailing near the front door. Beside her, Tante Marthe has tears streaming down her face.

"What is wrong?" I ask.

"Soldiers came. They have taken Manon," Tante Marthe manages to choke out. "They are rounding up Royalists, and our Manon has been declared one. They have taken her to prison."

"We have to do something," I say.

"But what?" Tante Anne-Marie asks. "She worked for the king. We cannot deny it."

"But she has never said she was for the king or against him," I protest, thinking back to Manon's guarded words on all subjects to do with the monarchy, her stated opinion that survival was all that mattered and that we should keep our loyalties to ourselves.

"It doesn't matter," Tante Anne-Marie cries. "Working for the king is enough to suspect she is for him."

"If l'Oncle were here, he would know what to do," Jean-Louis says.

He is right. Unfortunately, l'Oncle has been sent to the countryside by the new National Assembly to oversee obtaining food for the city. With the imprisonment of the king and the relinquishing of his position, many services have suddenly gone awry. Food is hard to obtain. Mail delivery is nonexistent.

"Well, he isn't here," Tante Marthe says, untying her apron and throwing it on a chair. "So it will be up to us to find out where they have put her, and get her out."

She strides toward the kitchen and comes back with a tricolor ribbon in her hair.

"Where are you going, sister?" Tante Anne-Marie asks.

"To find Manon," Tante Marthe says.

"What if they arrest you?" Jean-Louis cries.

"Don't be silly," Tante Marthe snaps. "If they meant to arrest me, they would have done it when they came for Manon. Even the revolutionaries aren't that unorganized."

"She'll never survive in prison," Tante Anne-Marie says, twisting her apron into knots.

"We'll find her and bring her food until we can get her out," I assure her.

Tante Anne-Marie looks at me. "You do not understand. Manon has an absolute horror of closed-in spaces. She will go mad in there."

Suddenly I understand why Manon snapped any time I said something that would have landed her in a cell. I remember her request that we move to a larger room within the prison when I was arrested, and how she slapped me in the carriage when I spoke treasonous words. All along, Manon has been afraid of being in a small space. Manon, who is always so strong, has a weakness, and I wish that I could free her from the terror she must be feeling in whatever prison they have committed her to.

"Enough," Tante Marthe says. "I am off to find out what has become of Manon. And I will not return until I have news."

With that, Tante Marthe sails off into the still dark streets of Paris, her jaw set, her wide form swaying back and forth as she marches away.

"*Mon Dieu*," Jean-Louis whispers. "I would not want to be Manon's jailer. Tante Marthe will beat him to death."

I cannot help it. In spite of the dire situation, I laugh. And soon, even Tante Anne-Marie gives a small smile of hope.

Ↄↄ

Tante Marthe returns late in the morning. She sighs and lowers her heavy frame into a kitchen chair. "She is at *Les Carmes*."

"That horrid place?" Tante Anne-Marie cries. "How is she surviving?"

"Not well," Tante Marthe says. "She was begging me to get her out, but there was nothing I could do. I tried to bribe the guards. But they kicked me out and told me not to come back, or they would imprison me, too. And there is word on the street that more people have been arrested, other people who are considered Royalists."

"What do they mean to do with them?" Tante Anne-Marie asks. "Will they keep them in prison indefinitely?"

"*Non*," Tante Marthe says, looking up at her sister. "They plan to assess if they are truly Royalists, and if they might be in league with the king's supporters."

Tante Marthe pauses and winces. "And if they find they are guilty, then they will execute them."

Ↄↄ

Tante Marthe, Jean-Louis, and I make our way slowly toward the prison of Les Carmes. Jean-Louis has insisted on carrying the basket of meat pies Tante Anne-Marie has made for her daughter. But his arms shake, and I worry that they will all go tumbling into the streets. I know the people walking by us would kill us if they knew what was in the basket; everyone fights for food these days. I can smell the lovely scent of pork every once in a while, and I hope that the aroma does not carry far in the wind.

At last, we reach the prison.

"You will have to go from here without me," Tante Marthe says, her eyes clouding over. "The guards will not let me in again. *Bonne chance.*"

Together, Jean-Louis and I go inside.

"What do you two want?" a guard in the front room asks. He has a patch over one eye, and a long, dirty beard.

"We are here to see Mademoiselle Manon Tussaud," I tell him.

"What's in the basket?" the guard asks.

"Food," Jean-Louis pipes up before I can warn him.

"*Bon*," the guard says, taking the basket from Jean-Louis. "I'm sure I'll enjoy whatever you've brought me."

"But that is for Mademoiselle Manon," Jean-Louis protests.

The guard grins at Jean-Louis. "Prisoners aren't allowed special deliveries."

He rises from his chair, after stashing our basket under his desk. "Come along, then. I'll take you to her."

Jean-Louis and I follow the guard down narrow, winding corridors. We pass cell after cell—small, airless, dark, and dank cubicles. At last the guard stops, pulls out a key, and unlocks one of the cell doors.

"Ten minutes," he tells us. "Then I'll be back for you."

I enter with Jean-Louis. Twenty women are sitting on straw in the dark, talking quietly. Manon is lying on the floor, curled into a ball. I go to her and touch her shoulder.

"Manon?"

She looks up, her eyes wild. She grabs onto my knees. "Celie, Celie, get me out of here. Get me out of here, please. You must get me out now."

The hopelessness of the situation hits me hard.

One of the women rises and walks over to me. "Is she your *maman*?"

I shake my head at the same time that Jean-Louis says, "*Oui*."

The woman looks at us curiously.

"She is like a mother, as we have none but her," Jean-Louis says, poking me.

Jean-Louis is right. Manon and l'Oncle and the aunts have become family to me; Manon is now a mother to us both.

"My name is Joséphine," the woman says. She holds out a slender hand, and I shake it. "Your *maman* is not doing well. She thinks she cannot breathe."

"She does not like to be in closed spaces," I say as Manon clutches at me, her fingers digging into my skin.

Joséphine nods. "Do not worry. We will watch over her."

The other women nod their heads, too.

"*Merci*," I say. "We had brought her some food, but the guard took it."

"We thank you for trying," Joséphine says. "We are lucky to get a few peas and beans to eat."

"Though they are so old, you can't chew them," a woman adds.

"Ah, well," Joséphine says, "at least we have each other."

"For the time being," another woman says. "But soon they will decide whether we are to live or die."

"If hunger doesn't kill us first," another woman says.

I listen to the words of these women, sitting in the dark, trying to keep their spirits up, and my anger rises. How can the effort to help the people of France have come to this?

Yes, Manon has worked for the king, but it was to earn a living, nothing more. How many of these women have also been wrongly imprisoned? I think of Paul Butterbrodt and the other entertainers. Will they, too, be considered Royalists, simply because they have provided entertainment for the wealthy? These people were the very commoners we believed in and argued for, and yet, here they are, still suffering. Some are worse off than before this fight for freedom.

How far will these revolutionaries go? Will they truly imprison anyone who has even come into contact with the royals?

I think of Algernon then. How can he condone this? How can he let this happen? For the first time ever, I do not regret refusing him, and I hope I will never see him again.

Chapter Fifteen

Three days later when Jean-Louis and I arrive, we find Manon fragile and feverish.

"She has been like this for two days now," Joséphine says. "And there has been no food brought to us since you left. We all grow weak."

No food? Nothing? It is unconscionable. They have not even found these women guilty of anything yet.

I am tired of standing by and doing nothing.

"We will bring you food tomorrow," I promise. "We will do it every day until you are each free from here."

"How can we do this, Celie?" Jean-Louis asks. "The guard will take it away."

"Some things, Jean-Louis, even a guard will not touch," I say.

⁓

The next day, Jean-Louis and I walk back toward the prison. In my arms, I carry the mold of the head of Mirabeau. Inside the head, I have hidden food—food that will not give off enticing aromas like Tante Marthe's pork pies, but simply bread and cheese and fruit.

In order to obtain this food, I had to sell the silver brushes and the china swan I once stole from Manon. The cheese is moldy, the fruit overripe, and the bread several days old, but at least these women will eat a bit today.

"Brought me something again?" the guard asks when we enter Les Carmes.

"*Non, monsieur*, I am sorry," I say. "We are out of food for the moment. But we need Mademoiselle Manon's help with one of our displays."

The guard eyes the head warily. "I'm not sure that is proper."

"Oh, *monsieur*," I exclaim, "you would not want to prevent us from displaying the image of the revolution's hero, Monsieur Mirabeau, would you? Mademoiselle Manon is the only one who can approve the right tint for his face.

"But of course," I add, holding out the head, "if you would like to examine it yourself first . . . ."

The guard draws back as if he has been bitten. "*Merci*. It is not necessary."

I give Jean-Louis a stern look to keep him from laughing. It pleases me to use Mirabeau to sneak food to Manon, just as he used my drawings to incite the violence that has brought us to this horrible place.

But my triumph at fooling the guard dies when we get to the cell. Three of the women have had their hair hacked short. One of them is Manon.

I know what that means.

Manon's hair has been cut short so that it will not catch in the blade of the guillotine. I have heard of this new instrument, but have not seen it in operation. The device sends a blade down upon a convicted criminal's neck, supposedly creating a more humane death than an executioner's beheading, as sometimes the executioner's sword goes astray, leaving the victim's head half on and half off. I cover my mouth to keep from vomiting.

"Celie?" Jean-Louis says in a small voice.

"I am sorry, *ma petite*," Joséphine says, coming forward. "They were here yesterday and made their decision. She is to face the guillotine in three days' time."

She puts her hand on my shoulder and an arm around Jean-Louis. "There is nothing you can do now, but be kind to her. Show her some love. She can carry that with her to the end."

I cannot believe this is happening. How can they convict Manon?

"You have brought her something?" Joséphine asks.

I turn to the kind woman. "We have food. It's not much, though."

I undo the towel that has been shoved into the bottom of Mirabeau's neck and pull out the bread and cheese.

"Oh, bless you, *ma petite*," Joséphine says, as she passes the food around the little prison cell. "Every little bit helps."

I hand the head to Jean-Louis and take some food over to Manon.

"Manon," I say, bending down, "come. You must eat."

Manon does not move, but her fevered eyes meet mine. They are black and empty, already half-dead. Then she looks over at Jean-Louis, and her eyes fall on the bust of Mirabeau. She makes a small sound of recognition.

"Jean-Louis," I say, hope rising in me at this sign of life in Manon, "bring the head to me."

Jean-Louis does as I ask. Manon takes the head from me and stares at it for a while. "Be sure to remind l'Oncle that Monsieur Mirabeau's mole had a tinge of black in it." Her voice cracks as she speaks, and her fingers shake as she points to the right side.

"*Oui*," I agree. "But now you must eat."

Manon's eyes glaze over again. "I am suffocating, Celie. I can't breathe in here. I am going to die."

"I know it is hard," I tell her, "but you can't give up. You must try, Manon, try to hold on."

"For what?" Manon asks. "The guillotine?"

She closes her eyes and turns her face away from me.

"I will get you out, Manon," I promise. My heart is so heavy I can barely speak. "I will get you out. Whatever it takes, I will get you out."

∽

"They cannot execute Manon," Jean-Louis says as we make our way back to the Boulevard du Temple. His face grows contorted with held-back tears. "Isn't there anything we can do to stop this?"

"I don't know," I say.

"Shall we tell Tante Marthe and Tante Anne-Marie?" Jean-Louis asks.

"We have to," I say. "We have no choice."

"Perhaps we could send a message to l'Oncle out in the country," Jean-Louis suggests. "He will have some contacts. Maybe he can get a reprieve for her."

"It will take too long, Jean-Louis," I say. "A rider could not get to l'Oncle and back in time for him to do all he would have to in order to rescue her."

"What can we do, then?" Jean-Louis asks. "Do you think Tante Anne-Marie or Tante Marthe might have an idea?"

"Be quiet, Jean-Louis," I snap. "I have to think."

I sit down on a stone step leading down to the Seine. I watch the river rolling slowly by. How many years has it been moving along like this, unchanged by all the turmoil people living on its banks have wrought? I want to throw myself into the river, turn on my back, and float away from all the chaos.

I know what I have to do, even though I do not want to. But it is Manon's only chance. I have not seen Algernon in over two months. Has he forgotten me already in his work for the National Assembly? Will he be able to soften his heart enough to help me if I go to him? Or will he make good on his threat to ignore me should I need his help?

I stand. I will have to try. I know now the only thing that matters to me—the only thing that has ever mattered to me—is family.

Life had been good when Maman and Papa and Jacques were alive. Life had been adventurous when Algernon and I were together and a team. Life has been lovely with Manon and l'Oncle and the aunts. Through all those times, it hasn't mattered who has been in charge or who has ruled the country. We might have been hungry, and we might have been homeless. But we had each other. I refuse to let Manon become one of the growing number of dead of the revolution. She is my family now, and I will fight tooth and nail to save her.

"Come along, Jean-Louis," I say, pulling him up from the step. "We have a ribbon to put on our door."

&

I pin the tricolor ribbon on the rough wooden frame. I pray that somehow, someway, Algernon still cares enough to have someone watching over me, keeping an eye on me should I need him. If no one comes by tomorrow, I will be forced to go looking for him myself, braving the chaotic streets and the powerful men of the National Assembly.

"Do you think he will come?" Tante Anne-Marie asks. Her eyes are red-rimmed from crying, her nose swollen, and she has not eaten in days.

"We will have to see," Tante Marthe says, taking her sister by the shoulder and steering her back toward the kitchen. "We will just have to wait."

I sit on the front steps, but by evening, Algernon has not come. Reluctantly, I go to bed. But I sleep fitfully, afraid that there will be a knock on the door, and I will not hear it.

The next morning, I wait on the front steps again. Tante Marthe brings me some clear soup with bits of mushroom she has managed to find. "He will not come any faster because you are sitting here. Work will make the time pass more quickly."

"If it goes faster," I snap, "Manon will be dead."

Tante Marthe says nothing more. She leaves me alone on the step.

An hour drags by, and then another. Around midday, a man comes to the bottom of the stairs. "You are Celie?"

"Who wants to know?" I ask.

"If you are Celie," the man says, "I am to take you with me."

Algernon has answered. He has cared enough to respond to my call for help.

"Tante Marthe," I yell into the house, "I am off to see Algernon."

The door to the house is opened quickly. Tante Anne-Marie stands there, tears in her eyes. "Oh, *ma petite*, please beg him to help my girl. Please."

"I will, Tante Anne-Marie," I promise. "I will be back soon with news."

I turn to follow the man. "I am ready."

And I am. I am ready to go to the boy I have turned against, and beg for the life of Manon.

❧

I am ushered into a building within the Palais-Royal. After all this time, it seems Algernon has not wandered far from our old haunts.

A door is opened and the young man waves his hand, indicating I am to enter. Inside, I find Algernon with two other men and a table on which rests a quill, some paper, and an inkwell. The men turn when I come into the room. Algernon immediately steps forward, but he does not embrace me.

"You have need of my services?" he asks formally, bowing to me instead.

His courtly manners confuse me. Has he brought me here only to make fun of me? Will he keep his promise to be there should I need him, or will he rebuff me in front of these strangers?

"I wish to speak in private, Algernon," I say, my voice barely above a whisper.

"There is nothing you can ask of me that cannot be asked before Monsieur Marat and Monsieur Robespierre," Algernon says.

I hesitate. I know these two gentlemen are leaders of the revolution. How can I beg for Manon in front of them? And how can Algernon ask this of me? Can he not see that I am nervous and afraid? I understand that he might refuse me, but I did not think that he would humiliate me in front of others. I stand there, his fool.

The men wait.

"Manon has been arrested," I say.

"I am aware of that," Algernon says. "She worked for the royals."

"She only did this to put food on her table," I protest. "She did not agree with the king. Le Salon du Cire is now the Museum of the People. L'Oncle is a National Guardsman. You made him one yourself. They have supported the new government. How can you imprison her and threaten her with death?"

"You are lucky you are not in there with her yourself," Algernon snaps. "She was *not* concerned with putting food on her table, but with putting money in her own pocket. And to do that, she used whatever and whoever she could—including you and me. She has acted no differently than the royals themselves."

"She has taken care of me, Algernon—and you," I argue. "She protected me and gave me a home. She gave you one, too, for a while, or have you forgotten?"

"Only so that she could keep you near her and use your drawing skills to further her own ambitions," Algernon says.

I want to snap that Algernon had done no differently, that in the way he is treating me now, I can see that he has never cared for me, but has used me, too.

But instead, I fall to my knees, willing to do anything to get him to see reason. "Please, Algernon, I beg of you. Let her go." I pause. "She is like a *maman* to me."

"*I* rescued you from the streets," Algernon snaps. "*I* kept you from starving. You should be *here* beside *me* as we take this great step in history. It should be *me* who has earned your love, not some woman who can do nothing but make heads."

"She is a person, Algernon," I argue. "All those you have imprisoned are people. People who did things, worked with the wealthy, just to keep from starving."

"They could have done more," Algernon argues. "They could have worked as we did to end this tyranny.

"Or I should say, as *I* did," he adds bitterly.

"It got violent," I say. "You know I cannot bear violence, Algernon."

Algernon nods. "Yes, a few have died. But fewer than would have if we had allowed the king to continue with his lavish ways, spending money that should have been used for the good of everyone. The people were starving, Celie. They deserved better from their leader."

I cannot argue with this. He is right. But can every individual be expected to have the strength to fight despotism? Aren't some born to be leaders, and others followers? These days, I do not want to lead. I only want to follow and survive.

"Manon will die tomorrow," Algernon says, his lips pressed tight. "And perhaps that will bring you to your senses about where your loyalties should lie these days."

"Enough."

The voice is strong. I look over. The man Marat has spoken. His eyes gleam at me in a way that makes chills run up and down my spine.

"This Manon?" Marat asks. "She is the woman Tussaud? The maker of the wax models at the People's Museum?"

"*Oui*," I answer.

Marat purses his lips for a moment and taps his finger against his cheek, as if deep in thought. Then he smiles.

"We will save your Manon, *ma petite*," Marat tells me. "Go home. I will write the order to free her today."

"Oh, Monsieur Marat, *merci, merci*." I say. I take his hand and plant it with kisses.

"But . . . ." he says, and pauses, smiling oddly at me.

"*Oui, monsieur?*" I ask, dread falling over me like a blanket.

"We will have need of her services," he says, "and soon. And there will be no denying us what we will ask of her. Do you understand, *ma petite?*"

I shiver. "What might that be?"

"It is none of your concern now," Marat tells me. "Just understand that her freedom does not come without a price. Will you take this deal? Are we agreed?"

I have no choice. "*Oui, monsieur*. We are agreed."

Chapter Sixteen

Tante Marthe carries Manon through the front doors of the house at the Boulevard du Temple. Her hair is dirty and stringy, and her eyes are unfocused. Her clothes hang loosely on her, and her face is gaunt. When he sees her, Jean-Louis cries. I hover by Manon's bedroom door, wondering if she will ever again be the same strong woman who rescued me from being hanged by the Comte d'Artois.

After two days of sleeping and being spoon-fed by Tante Anne-Marie, Manon emerges. I hear the distinguishable click of her heels on the wooden floors one morning and steel myself for the worst. Jean-Louis raises his head, like a dog that has heard his master.

Manon sweeps into the kitchen, trying to act as if nothing has transpired in the last few weeks, as if she had never faced execution. But I can see the dark circles under her eyes, and that her hands shake a bit.

"Both of you, eat up. We have much to do today." Manon's first words are firm and clear.

Jean-Louis lets out a cry of joy, jumps up from his place, and runs to hug her. She kisses the top of his head. I swallow hard, but the lump in my throat catches and stays there, forcing me to blink.

Manon pries Jean-Louis's fingers from her waist, taking his hand instead, and pulls him along until she comes to stand beside me. "I owe you my life, it seems."

"You rescued me," I say, shrugging.

Manon rests her hand lightly on my head. I can feel the softness of her fingers as they brush the hair from my forehead. For a minute, I am transported back to the farm and the tenderness of my own mother's hand.

"Still," Manon says, "it must not have been easy to beg Algernon for my life."

I know I should tell Manon that there will be a price to be paid down the road. But my throat closes up at the mention of Algernon. I can still picture his bitter eyes when the deal was made, and I hate that he has been disappointed not to see me suffer Manon's execution. I have won Manon's freedom, and lost Algernon for good. I, too, have paid a price.

"Why did you save me, Celie?" she asks.

"I wouldn't have had a place to sleep or eat if the museum closed, now would I?" I say.

Jean-Louis glares pointedly at me.

"Celie, why did you do it?" Manon repeats.

I bite my lip to stop from breaking down over all that has happened.

"Come, *ma petite*," Manon says. "You must stop always trying to be so strong. You have seen my weakness and saved me. Let me see yours."

My eyes meet hers, and my strength seems to flee from me. The tears I have denied for two years finally come. They are heavy and profuse, and I think they will never end. I cry for Papa and Maman and Jacques. I cry for Algernon, and Madame Élisabeth and the queen, and the sorry mess that has been made in the search for equality. I cry for Manon, who suffered much in prison. And I cry for myself, for all I have lost and all I have found, and all I am afraid will be taken from me again.

Manon reaches out and draws me to her, and I lean into her arms, smelling her lavender scent.

"I love you, Manon," I whisper.

"And I love you, too, *ma petite*," Manon returns. "We are family now, *non?*"

"Me, too," Jean-Louis cries, inserting himself between us.

Manon laughs, and I know she is right. I have found family again. I just hope that when the National Assembly comes to demand payment of us, it will be something Manon will forgive me for.

ↂ

L'Oncle comes back from the country with food and with news. "They are to put the king on trial."

I look up in shock from the drawing I have been doing. "What for?"

"Gamin, the locksmith who worked with the king at Versailles, led the revolutionaries to a concealed wall safe at the Tuileries in which papers were found that implicate the king in a plot to free the monarchy," l'Oncle tells us. "The revolutionaries have had the papers for some time, but have just decided to act on them."

I cannot believe that the locksmith of Versailles betrayed the king. The king had spent most of his time with the man. Did the man have no gratitude?

But then, it dawns on me. Would the king's locksmith not have been one of the first to be executed as a Royalist? Perhaps by turning these papers over to the revolutionaries, he saved his own neck.

"Impossible," Manon says. "Our king could no sooner organize a plot than Jean-Louis could."

"It doesn't matter," Jean-Louis whispers. "They do not really need a reason to put our king on trial."

I start at Jean-Louis's words. The little boy is growing up fast, and it saddens me to know that he needn't live in the streets to understand the madness that is surrounding us.

ↂ

It does not take long for the king to be found guilty and condemned to the guillotine. He is no longer the king but a simple citizen of France, stripped of his title. Soon Louis Capet, as he is now called, will die.

⁓

The day of the king's execution, the streets of Paris are silent. All the shops are closed, as are the windows of every house. A cold winter wind sweeps the streets of Paris, though the sun shines brightly. I huddle near Manon as we watch the closed coach carrying the king sweep by our home.

Others gather along the boulevard, weeping into their handkerchiefs. They turned their backs on their king, and now they are sad about it?

"We don't have to go, do we, Manon?" Jean-Louis asks, tears streaming down his face. "We don't have to go see him at the guillotine?"

"Of course not," Manon says, pulling Jean-Louis closer. "But I am glad you stood here to watch him go by."

"Perhaps he looked out and saw me," Jean-Louis says. "Perhaps he even knew me. Perhaps he said to himself, oh, there is the little boy who brought suitcases to my guest rooms at the Petit Trianon."

"*Oui*, perhaps he did, Jean-Louis," Manon says. "And even if he didn't, I am sure he was honored by the quiet and solemn way you watched him pass by."

Behind the king, another carriage comes down the boulevard, stopping short of our house.

Dismay sweeps over me, for the man who gets out of the carriage is the same man who came to get me the day I needed Algernon. He walks toward us, pausing just below our steps. "The time has come, Mademoiselle Celie. The National Assembly has need of your services."

Manon looks at me in confusion as the man turns toward her. "And of yours, *mademoiselle*," he adds, bowing.

I turn to Manon. "I didn't have a choice. I had to make a deal to free you."

"And exactly what was the deal you made, Celie?" Manon asks.

"I don't know," I babble. "They wouldn't tell me. They just made me promise that when they came for us, we would do as they said, no questions asked."

But I do know what they want. As soon as I saw the king's carriage roll by and the familiar man step from the one behind it, I knew. So does Manon.

"You would like me to bring my materials, I presume?" she asks, turning back toward the man, who stands tapping his foot impatiently.

"That would be wise," the man answers.

"I will get them and be with you in a minute," Manon tells him. "Celie, Jean-Louis, inside, please."

"She will come with you, *mademoiselle*," the man says.

"I believe I can handle this job on my own," Manon says.

"I am sure you can, *mademoiselle*, but my instructions were quite clear. The girl comes with you." The man glances over at Jean-Louis. "The boy can stay."

I let out the breath I have been holding. I cannot imagine how I would have felt if Jean-Louis had been forced to go with us to do our job. It would have broken his heart. Now, it will only break mine. But at least Manon will not have to do this on her own.

"We will be right back, then," Manon says. "Come, Celie. Help me gather the things we will need."

Inside, I stumble over myself to find the right words to apologize to Manon.

But before I can say much of anything, Manon whirls on me and grabs me by the shoulders, startling me. "Enough. You did what you had to. Did you think I would blame you? *Non, ma petite.* You have learned well. We have survived. The politics are nothing but nonsense. Survival is all. Remember that. Always."

Tante Anne-Marie comes down the stairs, her arms filled with laundry. "Has it happened then? Has he gone past?"

"*Oui*, Maman," Manon says, "but Celie and I have a job we must do now."

Tante Anne-Marie drops her bundle. "*Non.* They have not asked it of you?"

"They have," Manon says. "And so we shall comply. Please watch Jean-Louis for me. This will not be an easy day for him."

Tante Anne-Marie comes and puts her arms around her daughter. "Please don't go. What if something goes wrong? And how can *you* do this today? You *know* your king. You have spoken to him and worked for him. It is beyond belief that they would ask this of you."

"Nothing is beyond belief when there is a revolution and the future of a country with all its power at stake, Maman," Manon says.

Tante Marthe comes into the hallway, a bucket and mop in her hand. "Saw the king's coach roll by from the kitchen window. Poor man."

She stops. "What has happened?"

"Manon and Celie will be going to the execution," Tante Anne-Marie says. "They have been requested to do some work."

"*Mon Dieu*," Tante Marthe snaps. "We have traded fools for savages."

"No matter," Manon says. "We must not keep our escort waiting."

☙

As we roll up to the square where the king is to be executed, I look out at the crowd that has gathered. They are a large group, but somber and quiet. At least, they seem bent on giving the king some respect in the final moments of his life.

The guillotine looms large on the scaffold. Its blade glints in the sunlight. I turn my head.

"Out you go," the man orders us.

Manon and I descend from the carriage. Manon wraps her arms around me. "Shut your eyes. It will be over quickly."

"*Non,*" says the man who is with us. "Everyone here must witness the event."

"We are doing what you have asked of us," Manon snaps. "But we will do it in the *manner* we want."

"You will not, *mademoiselle,*" the man says, "for if you both do not watch, I will take you back to prison."

"It's all right, Manon," I say, remembering Manon's words on surviving. "I am a good patriot. I can do this."

The king mounts the steps of the scaffold. He has on simple clothes, but he walks as if he is wearing the royal ermine robes to which he is accustomed. Louis XVI holds his head high, and his eyes are steady as he looks out at the crowd. At Versailles, he had seemed such a simple and lonely man. But today, he is a king.

He steps forward and opens his mouth. I wait, wanting to hear what he has to say to us, hoping his words will be of forgiveness. But at that moment, the captain of the guard makes a motion, and the drums begin to beat. The king's words are lost in the noise.

Louis XVI closes his mouth and gives a slight smile. Two men come forward and help him to his knees. The king looks out at his people once more, then lets himself be strapped below the blade of the guillotine.

The executioner steps forward and pulls the lever. With a loud whoosh, the blade comes tearing down from its position high above the king. In less time than it takes me to cover my mouth, the king's head is severed from his body. His head rolls forward into a bucket that has been placed there to catch it. Blood shoots from the headless torso, spattering those who stand at the front of the crowd.

The people rush forward, dipping handkerchiefs or pieces of cloth into the blood of the king. The executioner lifts the head from the bucket and holds it up for everyone to see. But there is no cheering. Instead, people weep, and for that, I am glad. Perhaps the people's lack of enthusiasm for the king's beheading will end this. France can recover and go on as a republic.

The executioner begins to cut away at the king's hair, slipping locks of it into his pockets. Later, he will sell these locks of hair to anyone who wants to have a souvenir of the event. I know it is his right as the executioner, but that does not make it less gruesome.

"Come," the man says. "They will be bringing Louis Capet's body to La Madeline. You may do your job there."

He helps Manon and me back into the carriage. I am not sorry to leave the *Place de la Republique*, but I know what lies ahead will be worse.

&

When the king's head and body are finally delivered by three men to the cemetery, he has been stripped naked.

"Where are his clothes?" Manon snaps.

"The executioner took the buttons. We took the rest. They have been burned. And Louis Capet will be buried in limestone naked, without a coffin, so no one may raise him up again as a protest," Algernon says as he walks up to the churchyard grounds.

I wish he had not come.

"It's indecent to have him like this," Manon says.

"Feeling sorry for royalty?" Algernon asks, his eyes narrowing.

"*Non*, it wouldn't matter to me if he was a thief," Manon says, looking pointedly at Algernon. "I'd still prefer not to have a naked man placed before me."

"Not your choice, *mademoiselle*," Algernon says.

"But it is yours," she says, waving a hand toward me as I try my best not to look at the king.

Algernon has the good grace to redden at Manon's words, and I am glad that some decency remains deep within him. He undoes his jacket and lays it over the body. "Now, be about your business."

Manon reaches down and picks up the king's head. "Remember the governor of the Bastille," she whispers to me. "It is no different than that."

But Manon is wrong. It *is* different this time. Making a wax head from a beheaded stranger is terrible, but making a wax head from someone you have known alive is worse.

I keep thinking that the king will open his eyes and suddenly start speaking, asking me how I unlocked his doors, what he has done wrong.

And having Algernon standing there, watching me, makes it all the worse. How can he watch me do this? Has he never cared for me at all? Where is the kindness he once showed me? Bitterness nips at me.

"You aren't having trouble, Celie, are you?" Algernon asks. "You do appreciate the favor you have been granted, to make the wax head of the king, don't you? It will bring in much money to your precious museum, and I know how much that means to you and Mademoiselle Manon. Of course, first you will lend it to us, and it will travel throughout France, so everyone may see their late king."

My insides turn at his words. I bite back a sob. Why is he being so mean? Who is this cruel boy who stands before me now? How can he be the same boy I once loved so much?

Algernon bends down to look at me. I stare back at him defiantly.

His green eyes harden. "Crying for him, are we? That's not very patriotic, Celie."

"*Non*, Algernon," I whisper, looking at the poor king lying before me. "I am not crying for Louis Capet. I am crying for you, for what you have become."

"I am who I always was," he snaps.

I raise my eyes to meet his. "*Non*, you're not. I don't know *who* you are anymore."

We stare at one another, until finally, Algernon drops his gaze. He rises and turns, walking away into the darkness that is descending in the graveyard. He does not look back.

Chapter Seventeen

We finish casting the king's head. Manon treats it with the greatest of respect. I follow her lead, trying not to think about what I am doing, or about Algernon walking away.

Manon rises and turns to the three men who are left. "Come to the house in two weeks' time. It will be ready for you then."

The man who brought us here leads us from the graveyard. I look over my shoulder and see the two other men begin digging up dirt, preparing the unmarked, unadorned grave for the king.

It is over. The monarchy in France is ended.

ço

The months that follow are utter chaos. Extra taxes are imposed, ones that are in addition to the taxes we already paid under the king. There are daily food riots. The few *livres* people are able to earn are worth less and less, buying fewer and fewer of the scarce items that can be found. Raids are conducted on homes, often in the middle of the night, to ensure that no one is hoarding food. A new calendar and a new way to tell time are created. The new systems confuse everyone. And anyone who speaks out against the National Assembly is quickly imprisoned and executed. A reign of terror rules.

Manon insists that we go out as little as possible. I am not sorry for this enforced imprisonment. The streets terrify me—violence is an everyday occurrence now, and people often disappear without warning. Every time Tante Anne-Marie or Tante Marthe go off in search of food, I hold my breath until they return safe and sound.

The man Marat, who freed Manon from prison, is murdered. Even the leaders of the revolution have begun to turn on one another

My only solace is work. Drawing and making models soothes me. It helps me block out all the horror that surrounds us.

Then, one day, there is a knock at the door. To my surprise, Algernon's man is there again.

"What do you want?" I ask.

"We have need of your services," he says. "The queen is to go on trial."

"*Non,*" I say. "We did as you asked. We made the king's head. You paraded it around the country. We owe you no more."

"You owe your country nothing more?" the man asks, raising his eyebrows.

And once again, we are to face the horror of this revolution.

&

The queen is found guilty and beheaded just like her husband. We make a mold of the queen's head as the chilly autumn winds shake the few leaves still left on the trees. I cannot help but remember the woman I saw at the Petit Hameau, dancing with her ladies-in-waiting and making daisy chains in the summer sunshine. How silly it all seems now, as I look at the queen's dead blue eyes staring up at me.

"Celie?" Manon whispers.

I have missed a spot with the plaster. I take my brush and fill it in with shaking hands.

&

And then there is a lull, a blessed, wonderful lull. Food is still scarce, but order seems to have returned. Violence is less prevalent, and I begin venturing out again. Spring comes to Paris. Flowers poke their leafy stems from the earth. Leaves pop out from dark, bare branches. Lilacs release their sweet scent into the air.

I take a deep breath as I make my way back to the Boulevard du Temple, a fresh baguette under my arm. Perhaps, I think, spring will bring about a new world. Perhaps the old one of blood and hatred will be washed away in all this newness.

But as I round a corner, my hopes are dashed. The man who has come to get us before stands once again on the stairs. Above him, in the doorway, Manon has a hand to her chest. I run toward the house.

"What do you want?" I demand of him when I reach them.

The man gives me a crooked smile. "Your country has need of you again."

Manon is swaying, and her face is a ghostly white. I cannot imagine what the man might have said to shake the implacable Manon, but it does not matter. I will kill this man myself before I will do more work for him.

I sweep past him and stand in front of Manon. "*Non*, we are done. We have given enough. Go find someone else to sculpt your grisly heads."

"There is no one else, and you have no choice," the man says.

I almost choke at his words. The man is right. We cannot fight back without risking Manon's life, my own life, perhaps even Jean-Louis's, the aunts', and l'Oncle's lives.

I close my eyes in despair. "Fine. We will come. Who is it?"

"Madame Élisabeth," I hear the man say.

⁊

I can see that Manon is unsteady on her feet as we make our way to the Temple prison. My thoughts whirl in confusion. I have said we will do this, but how can we? I had not known the governor of the Bastille except by sight. I had known the king and queen, but only by seeing them at Versailles. Now I am to sculpt a person whom I not only know, but whom I admire? Will this nightmare never end?

When we enter Madame Élisabeth's room in the Temple prison, we find her on her knees, praying. Her hair has been hacked to her chin. She is dressed in a simple black gown. She rises when we enter the room.

Manon takes one look at Madame Élisabeth and turns away, a handkerchief to her mouth.

"*Madame*," I say, my voice shaking. I manage to sweep into a deep curtsy.

"Eh, no need for that," the jailer protests, pulling me back up. "She is Élisabeth Capet now. Do not bow and scrape for her."

"I didn't do it for her," I tell the man, wrenching my arm away. "I did it for me. I have always done it for myself."

The jailer scowls. "Be that as it may, you'll not kowtow on my watch. Thirty minutes now, no more."

I nod and watch as the jailer leaves us.

Madame Élisabeth embraces me. "I am glad that you have come."

"I wish . . . ." I begin.

"The time for wishing is over," Madame Élisabeth interrupts. "There is only time for *prayers* now."

I nod.

"Manon?" Madame Élisabeth says.

Manon puts out a hand signaling to give her a moment. When she turns around, her face is composed.

"*Madame*," she says, curtsying. But then, she sinks to the floor and begins to weep.

"*Non, non*," Madame Élisabeth says, sliding down next to Manon. "Enough of this, *mon amie*. This has nothing to do with you. I know that."

I cannot believe the strength Madame Élisabeth is showing. She is to be executed, and yet here she is, comforting Manon.

Madame Élisabeth looks up at me. "What news do you have of my niece and nephew? They have separated us. Have you heard anything of them?"

"They will not let you see them?" I ask.

Madame Élisabeth shakes her head. "*Non.*"

I frown. "They are all right. They are being schooled in revolutionary ideas, and that may save them yet."

Madame Élisabeth gives a little laugh. "The king's children? Revolutionary patriots?

"Well," she adds, patting Manon on the back, "as long as they are well, I can face this with peace. Now come, Manon. Tell me how I am to be displayed."

Manon shakes her head, still unable to speak.

"You are to be shown in your cell," I say. "That is why we are here."

"Then draw, child," Madame Élisabeth says. "Draw well this prison so that my people will see how I ended my life. And I will sit with Manon."

I do as commanded by the king's sister. I pull out my drawing tools and begin to sketch the wretched place in which Madame Élisabeth now resides. It is not hard, for there is little in the room.

But in a few days' time, we will have to make her death mask. And while I know that Madame Élisabeth will not survive, the question is, will Manon?

&

When the news of Madame Élisabeth's guilty verdict reaches the Boulevard du Temple, Manon takes to her bed and refuses to come out. I bring her a simple quiche, but the food remains on the table untouched.

"Is she any better?" Jean-Louis asks when I return to the kitchen.

I shake my head.

Tears slip down Jean-Louis's cheeks. I put my arms about the little boy.

"First Papa, and now Madame Élisabeth," Jean-Louis whispers. "Shall we lose Manon also?"

His words bring me up short. I saved Manon from prison, but if Manon goes mad sculpting Madame Élisabeth's head, what will it matter?

୧৩

Once more, I pin the tricolor ribbon to our front door. Then I sit upon the stoop. This time, I do not have to wait long. Algernon's man appears within an hour.

He bows to me, grinning. "You have need of something, *mademoiselle*? Perhaps you would like a few more victims for your museum?"

"I need to see Algernon," I say, ignoring the man's attempt at humor.

"About what?" the man asks.

"It's personal," I tell him.

The man shrugs. "Come along, then. I will take you to him."

I follow the man down narrow alleys and winding streets. This time, we do not end at the Palais-Royal, but instead enter a small apartment building near the Temple prison.

Inside one of the apartments, Algernon sits at a table, eating roast chicken, his head bent over his meal. He has not heard me come in, and so he does not look up.

My mouth waters with the smell of the meat and its rosemary seasoning. At the same time, anger rises strong and hot within me. Meat has been the scarcest item to obtain since the revolution, and I have to bite my tongue to keep from asking if he thinks all the people of Paris are enjoying a repast as fine as this.

"Hello, Algernon," I finally say.

His eyes widen when he looks up and sees me. Quickly, he wipes his mouth with a napkin. His hair is tousled, his cheeks flushed. He is even more handsome than I remember—and so impossibly distanced from the boy I once knew.

"I've come to ask you to relieve Manon and me from having to make a death mask of Madame Élisabeth," I say.

Algernon snorts. He picks up his chicken leg again and takes a bite. "Impossible. The people need to understand and see that she is dead."

"The people," I say, "need to see that their new government cares for *them*. They do not need these senseless, vengeful killings."

"Vengeful, are they, Celie?" Algernon asks. "Then so be it. Why should they continue to live when their luxuries took so many lives in starvation and taxes?"

I look pointedly at the chicken in front of Algernon.

Algernon lets out a guffaw. "This is hardly the palace of Versailles."

"*Oui*," I agree. "What the palace of Versailles represents is gone, as are most of those who inhabited it at one time. Their ghosts have been buried under a layer of lime, their heads severed from their bodies. I have seen it, Algernon. Or have you forgotten?"

Algernon stands up so quickly that his chair falls over. "Have *I* forgotten? It is you, Celie, who has forgotten. You have forgotten the streets and your *maman* and *papa*, your brother and . . . ."

He pauses. I know he is thinking of his beaten, dead Julia. I wish not to hurt him, but I cannot spare him the pain when so much is at stake.

"Maman and Papa and Jacques were not *just* about taxes and starvation and death," I tell him. "They were also about love, Algernon. Love. I'm sure Julia was, too."

There. I have said it—to his face. The ghost between us has a name and a shape at last.

"They would have hated all this beheading," I add. "They would have hated the way you are killing in the name of freedom. They would not have wanted the fight for equality to turn into this."

"You don't know that," Algernon snaps at me. "You can't possibly know what Julia would have thought."

I have encroached on his sacred memory. But I must go on.

"Oh, but I do," I say firmly. "They loved us, Algernon. Julia loved you. My family loved me. That is all they wanted, Algernon—love: to live good, honest, caring lives, to put food on the table, to have a roof over their heads, and to come home to us and live peacefully. That is what love is, Algernon. It is *not* about beheading those who wronged them."

"So you are the expert on love?" Algernon says mockingly. "Are you trying to tell me that you know love better than me? Do you think I don't know love?"

I hesitate. The boy who saved me from death, the boy who rescued every abandoned animal he found—that Algernon knew love. But the man who commanded me to make molds from the heads of the dead? The man who accepted so much violence? The man who stands before me now?

"Once," I finally say. "Once I think you knew how to love, to care. But now . . . ."

I stop and let the silence speak for me. We stare at each other.

"Now you are empty of it, Algernon," I finally say.

He turns away from me, and I know in that moment that I have failed to grant Madame Élisabeth—to grant *Manon*—her reprieve. But could I be less than honest with this boy I once cared about so deeply? In asking him to face what he has become, how can I, the girl whom he rescued from death with such compassion, not be the one to hold up the mirror and show him that he has lost his way?

Yet now, Manon will be forced to mold her dead friend's head, and despair over this knowledge leaves me almost breathless.

But when Algernon turns back around and looks full at me, I am surprised by what I see in his face—guilt, misery, even pain. He slowly picks up his overturned chair and sits back down. He buries his head in his hands.

"I am not proud of what I have done," he says softly.

"Then why did you do it?" I ask, and even I can hear the condemnation in my voice, the unyielding sound of it.

Algernon looks up at me with anguished eyes. "I was forced to it. It was out of my hands. I did not want this."

My heart softens a bit in my chest.

"The men in charge have made all these decisions," he whispers, his voice shaking. "And I have been made to support them. I had no choice."

I seize up again with anger. "You did have *some* choices. You did not need to be so cold-hearted when you came to the cemetery with the dead king. You had the ability to be kind that day, Algernon, but you were not."

"I came to offer you support," he says, anger rising in his voice to match mine. "I came to be with you, to comfort you. But you looked at me with such disdain that evening, as if I were no more than dirt on your shoe."

"What you were forcing me to do was unspeakable," I spit at him.

"I did not force you," he argues. "It was you who came here, begging for Manon's life. It was you who made the bargain. You, too, have been forced to do their bidding. So we are not so different, are we?"

Now Algernon holds the mirror to my face, forcing me to see the truth. I have been blaming him for the predicament I am in, but I suddenly realize that he is right. I also had a choice, and I chose to make a deal with the devil.

I look at him with new understanding. How many bargains has my rogue of a friend been forced to make?

"That does not excuse the ill way you have treated me," I say, unwilling to bend just yet.

Algernon gives a bitter laugh. "And what of the way you have treated me?"

"What do you mean?" I say, bewildered by this new turn of talk. "I have always had your interests at heart, and I have always been there for you."

"When you were at Versailles, were you there for me then?" he asks. "You left me, Celie, for two long months. And when I was made to do these things in order to have some ability to effect change, you were not there for me to confer with. I swore I would never get close to anyone again after Julia, but I did with you. And you abandoned me when I needed you most."

"I was working," I protest. "I was making drawings for Mirabeau."

"You did not need to go to Versailles for that," Algernon says. "There was plenty of wealth to draw here in Paris. And when you did go, it was I who had to prompt you to send some communication. Why did you abandon me?"

He gazes at me, pain and anguish etched deep into his face. And it is as if a light has fallen on me. How could I not have seen this? How can I not have understood? Like Julia, I left him. But Julia died. I did not.

I could have refused to go to Versailles. But was there not a part of me that wanted to be caught up in that world of luxury and privilege? To see it all close at hand?

"I knew there would be some violence," Algernon says almost to himself, and I hear the desperation in his voice, his need to puzzle it out, to understand what has happened to him. "There is no way to liberate a country without some loss of life. And yes, I wanted no more monarchy. I wanted to emulate the Americans, to have a system where the people choose their leaders. When the king and his family were imprisoned, I thought it for the best. We could rule ourselves. There was no need for a king to guide us. But to put him on trial? To behead him? To behead them all, so senselessly, now that they were rulers no more?"

Algernon shakes his head over and over as if he cannot believe the horror of it all. Now before me once more is the boy with whom I lived in alleys and broke the law in order to survive. He goes on, still sounding mystified. "I did not wish any of that. I did not want those terrible things to happen. But I was in too deep then. And there was no way to escape. And you had made your choice. You had chosen *her*. I had to carry on alone, unsure."

Algernon's disillusionment wraps itself around my own crushed hopes for something better, something finer for the people of France. We stand here now, both our dreams of equality consumed by the hatred and fear and violence of a revolution that has left us divided and bereft of spirit.

He gazes up at me with eyes almost black with despair. "Do you think me a monster then, Celie?"

Who can say what a monster is? A king so separated from his people that he can't see their pain? A girl so enamored of her art and her position that she abandons the very person who saved her life? Or a boy so caught up in a cause that he lets himself do things he will forever regret?

He is Algernon, my Algernon. And we are all capable of thoughtless deeds. I will not be the one to cast this stone.

"*Non*, Algernon," I say softly. "I do not think this."

"I do not understand how this has gotten so out of control," Algernon says. The bewilderment in his face makes my heart lurch. His pain is my pain once again. "I meant well. I truly did. But somehow it has turned out so very wrong."

I nod, tears in my eyes, thinking of Manon's words to me after the violence in the Place Vendôme. I think not only of the revolution and its horrible beheadings, but also of the king and

Madame Élisabeth, who had been unable as rulers to bring about change.

"I cannot stop her execution, even if I wanted to," Algernon says, looking up at me, his voice cracking. "I do not hold that high a position."

"Then spare me this, Algernon," I beg him, kneeling down in front of him. "You can at least spare me this."

"Spare Manon, you mean?" he says with bitterness.

I grab his hands, lace my fingers with his. We may be disillusioned, but we do not need to be defeated. There is a road back to each other. We can find it. "*Oui*, Algernon. I care for Manon, and the aunts, and l'Oncle. It is true. But how could you think I have stopped caring for you? Love has no limits, Algernon. Mine is infinite."

"I have missed you, Celie," Algernon whispers, pulling me close to him, his breath soft and hot on my skin.

"Then come back with me," I urge him, gripping his shirt in my fists. "Come back, and we can be together. Leave all this behind. We can ride this out. Manon will welcome you back, and I will never leave you alone again. I promise."

Algernon shakes his head. "I cannot. I have been too long with them. They would arrest and kill me."

He is right. I know he is right. If he walks away, the revolutionaries will have no choice but to declare him a Royalist and execute him. But how am I to bear this?

"Revolution is a hard thing," Algernon whispers, "a very hard thing to get right."

Still kneeling before him, he kisses the top of my head, and I let out a little sigh through choked-back tears.

"I relieve you of this duty," he says, clearing his throat and rising from his chair. "I will employ a balladeer to tell of her beheading instead. I will tell the Council that the wax could not be obtained in time."

I cannot speak for love and gratitude. I rise too, and place a hand on his chest, feeling the warmth of it and the beating of his heart as we stand together.

"Now, you must go," Algernon says, "for I have work to do."

"*Non*. I cannot leave you," I protest.

"You have no choice," Algernon says, closing his eyes. "Even with the mistakes that have been made, we must press on. France must be stabilized."

He barks for his man to come, and within seconds, the man is at the door.

"Please, Algernon," I beg him.

He pulls me toward him. He strokes my cheek, lets his fingers linger on my lips. Then ever so slowly, he bends and gently puts his lips to mine. At last!

I kiss him back with all the love I feel for him, and he wraps his fingers in my hair, draws me closer, kisses me more deeply.

Then he finally breaks from me and puts his lips to my ear. "I love you, Celie, far more than I ever loved her."

I stand speechless at this unexpected declaration.

Before I can respond, he is pushing me away from him.

"Take her," he commands the man.

"*Non*," I cry.

"*Au revoir*, Celie," Algernon says, turning so I can no longer look him in the eye.

And I am spirited away before I can even think how to fight my way back.

Chapter Eighteen

I cannot eat or sleep. I toss and turn in my bed and barely speak. Algernon has rescued me when I needed him most. How can I not do the same for him? But what am I to do?

The day of Madame Élisabeth's execution arrives. The world is bathed in soft spring sunshine.

"She shouldn't die alone," Manon says. "I must go and be with her at the end."

"I will come with you," I say, though I am tired and shaky these days, and do not know how much more I can bear without losing my own mind.

"I am coming, too," Jean-Louis pipes up.

"*Non*, Jean-Louis, you are too young," Manon says.

"She was there for *me* when my *papa* died," Jean-Louis argues, his lower lip trembling. "You cannot stop me from being there for *her*."

"He is right, Manon," I tell her wearily. "Jean-Louis loves Madame Élisabeth."

Reluctantly, Manon nods her head.

❧

The crowd is smaller than those that gathered at the executions of the king and queen. I pray this means that the people's need for revenge against their sovereigns will, like a fire washed by blood, soon be extinguished.

The drums begin to roll, and Madame Élisabeth climbs the stairs to the guillotine. She is dressed simply, her hands clasped before her.

Manon moves closer to the platform so that Madame Élisabeth might see us, and Jean-Louis bows to her.

Madame Élisabeth's eyes light up when she sees us standing there. Then she bends her head in prayer. The executioner gives her a few moments, then he nudges her and points toward the guillotine.

Madame Élisabeth smiles sadly. "*Merci*," she mouths.

She is strapped to the contraption, her head put in place.

I do not watch the end, but I hear the swish of the blade and the thump as it hits the wood. I hear Jean-Louis cry out, but not one other soul makes a sound. Silence reigns at Madame Élisabeth's death.

Finally, I open my eyes, but I cannot look at the scaffold. I cannot believe that Madame Élisabeth is truly gone.

Jean-Louis is in Manon's embrace.

I can think of nothing now but home and bed, and the sweet release of sleep. I long to sit next to Jean-Louis tonight, with a fire and l'Oncle reading to us as Manon sews or works on an exhibit.

Then, suddenly, I hear it—a tapping. I whirl around, my eyes searching wildly for Algernon's tall body and brown-haired head. But he is nowhere to be seen. Have the day's events unhinged my mind? Have I only imagined it?

"Celie?" Manon asks.

"Sssh," I command her.

There. There it is, once again. I listen to the tapping, translating as fast as the beats ring out.

"Celie, what is it?" Manon asks.

Tears fill my eyes, as I think of the young prince and princess still in prison. "There will be no more royal beheadings. They are done. Finished."

Finally, I think, the people of France can once more turn their thoughts to living. The dying is over.

My heart beats with gratitude to Algernon for letting me know this good news after such a horrendous day. I feel his love for me as if it is his own strong arms wrapping around me, and the pain of not being with him now is all the greater, as I feel his obvious concern for my well-being.

But then, the tapping starts again. I hold still, listening. The weight that has been in my chest lifts as I translate his message.

Go home. Wait for me there, he taps to me. *I will come for you tomorrow. I have a plan.*

He is coming. Tomorrow. He has a plan.

I turn and take Manon and Jean-Louis each firmly by the arm. "Come," I say. "We must hurry home."

❧

I wait the next day. Impatience burns inside me.

"What has got you so distracted?" Tante Marthe grumbles when I spill Jean-Louis's glass of milk, and the cup shatters as it hits the floor.

I cannot tell her, for I do not know when Algernon will be here, or what he will have planned when he does come. Will he ask me to leave Manon, Jean-Louis, and the aunts and uncle behind? If that is his plan, how am I to choose? Will he ask me to keep our flight secret? Will I have to slink away, like a shadow in the night? How can I leave these people who have become so dear to me? And yet, how can I not go with Algernon, should he ask it?

I dig my nails into the palms of my hands with worry as I work in the museum.

"*Mon Dieu*, Celie," l'Oncle snaps. "Where is your head?"

If I weren't so consumed with uneasiness, I would have to laugh at l'Oncle's question. Heads are everywhere here. Why ask where one is?

But my future with Algernon is no laughing matter. If we do flee, where can we go? Hiding is a temporary fix only. Eventually, the National Assembly will find us. We have no family outside France to protect us.

"Celie!" l'Oncle snaps.

I am brought out of my reveries. "I'm sorry, *mon oncle*," I say. "I think Madame Élisabeth's death has me on edge."

L'Oncle's eyes soften. "*Mais oui.* You are right. I was foolish to think work would ease your pain. Go. Rest. We can take this up when you are feeling better."

I leave, a liar for misleading him. Madame Élisabeth's death still distresses me, but it is Algernon's face that haunts me. I go to my room and pace. When will he come? What will he say?

By dinner, he is still not here. I go to the kitchen, but cannot eat. I excuse myself and go back to my room to renew my worrying.

Manon pokes her head in. "Celie, are you ill?"

When I shake my head, she sighs. "I wish you would tell me what is wrong."

But my throat is closed tight.

By midnight, I am still alone in my room and am forced to face the fact that he is not coming, that something or someone has prevented him from being here.

I remove my shoes, roll down my stockings, and prepare for bed. I lie staring out into the dark. Have they found him out? Has he been arrested? How can I lie here, not knowing what has become of him? How can I sleep, knowing he may even now be in a cell somewhere? But there is nothing I can do. No one I can turn to. I no longer have friends in places that could get me answers.

Eventually, I fall into an uneasy sleep.

I am awakened by a strange noise, and a hand is suddenly over my mouth.

I am about to scream, when I realize that before me is the face I have longed for all day.

He smiles.

"Algernon," I whisper when he drops his hand from my lips.

I bury my face in his chest, breathe in the smell of Paris on him.

"I can't stay long," he says.

"Why not?" I ask.

He grimaces. "A man has been watching me. It took all my considerable cunning to give him the slip and make my way here."

"Do they realize you were lying when you said we could not mold Madame Élisabeth's head for lack of material?" I ask, my throat thick with fear. Have I caused Algernon to be noticed by the Assembly in a way that could endanger him?

He shakes his head. "*Non*, but I have been arranging a ship and transport to England. Perhaps they have noticed my extended absences."

He has said it. We are to go to England. I pray that no one involved in his escape plans has talked. But I say nothing. We both know the risks.

He stands. "You must gather your things over the next few days, Celie. We will have to slip away as soon as the weather turns for the worse."

"The worse?" I repeat, my mind racing ahead to Manon and Jean-Louis, my heart in my throat as I consider leaving them behind.

"There is talk of rescuing the young prince and princess," Algernon says. "They have blockaded part of the river, looking for any who would help restore the monarchy by putting the young prince on the throne."

I consider this. "Then how will we set sail?"

Algernon grins. "As we have many times before. By our wits."

He strides toward the door. "Now I must go. Be ready, though."

"Algernon," I say, "be careful."

"Aren't I always?" he asks.

He pauses. "You have not asked about Manon or Jean-Louis."

I shake my head. "*Non.* Though I will miss them, I will go with you."

He laughs, a laugh so loud that I am sure it will wake the whole household. His eyes are dancing with merriment. "I am delighted with your devotion, Celie, but you need not have made that choice, for they are coming with us."

"Truly?" I ask, barely able to believe in this miracle.

"Truly," he says. "I saw Dr. Curtius before I came up here. How did you think I got in?"

He laughs loudly again, and then he is gone.

And I am left to enjoy the way he has played me.

Then I pause. For although we are escaping, we have not avoided the guillotine just yet.

☙

Several days later, rain pierces the night as we slip from the house at 20 Boulevard du Temple. The weather has now worsened.

Dr. Curtius and the aunts are to stay behind and watch over the People's Museum. They were never at Versailles, and Dr. Curtius is providing food to the National Assembly from contacts he has. The risk of death for them is minimal. For Manon, Algernon, and myself, the danger is constant, and I will not leave Jean-Louis behind.

There is no moon, and so the night is black. Wind whips through the streets of Paris, but nothing else occupies these alleyways. The National Assembly has imposed a curfew that has left everyone indoors, and our footsteps are loud in the eerie emptiness. Where once these streets would have been filled with the sounds of laughter and gaiety, they are now deserted and silent.

We slip from building to building like shadows. But our progress is slow. While Algernon and I could have fled fleetly on foot, Manon in her corset and Jean-Louis with his little legs slow our pace maddeningly. When we reach the walls of the city,

Algernon palms the guard some coins. The man turns his back as we slip out to a waiting wagon. We climb up, and though the horses Algernon has paid for are old and slow, we move more quickly than on foot.

I begin to breathe more easily. Then, behind us in the distance, I see a line of light.

"Algernon," I whisper, "men with lanterns on horseback."

He turns and looks over his shoulder, and I see his face go white. He flicks the whip across the horses' backs, but they move no faster.

"Algernon?" I say.

"We aren't far," he says, but his voice is tight, and already I can see the line of light is drawing nearer.

At last I hear the sound of water, and in the darkness and the rain and the fog I can just make out a vessel lying at anchor out on the Seine. But along with the lapping of waves, I can also hear the pounding of hooves getting closer.

Algernon stops the wagon. He climbs out and swings Manon down, then lifts Jean-Louis to the ground. A small skiff awaits us at the dock, and Manon and Jean-Louis run toward it over the wet cobblestones. The sailor waiting for us is already signaling that he means to leave in quick order and will abandon us if we do not hurry.

We must not be caught. We would all be executed for our attempt at escape, but if the Assembly learns who we are, even Dr. Curtius and the aunts will suffer.

Algernon reaches up his arms for me just as a shot rings out. He stumbles, and I fall upon him.

"*Dépêchez-vous! Dépêchez-vous!*" the sailor calls, urging us to move quickly.

I grab Algernon's arm and pull him to his feet. Together we run for the boat as more shots ring out. The horses are coming at us fast.

We scurry aboard, and the sailor begins to row frantically. The skiff slides away from shore at a frustratingly slow pace. The riders arrive at the water's edge. But the fog has grown heavier now, and at last, we are too far into the river for them to reach us. We are free.

I almost weep with relief. Once again, Algernon and I have slipped the grasp of those who would see us jailed.

I turn to him, smiling. And then I see his face, drawn and gray, and that he clutches his side. He slumps over, and I am upon him in a flash, moving his hand away so that I see it—the hole, the blood.

Chapter Nineteen

When we reach the boat that will transport us to the channel and on to England, we carry Algernon below. Manon rips apart his shirt and probes the wound. Blood flows out. And I have to steady my thoughts, or I will faint.

Can I have come this far only to lose him now?

"Is it bad?" I ask, my voice shaking.

Manon doesn't answer. "Fetch my waxwork bag, Jean-Louis. Celie, ask one of the sailors above to give you a pail of hot water, clean cloths, and a bottle of alcohol, whatever they may have."

Jean-Louis hurries to do as Manon bids, but I stand there, rooted as an oak. I do not want to leave him.

"Celie," Manon barks at me.

Algernon moans.

"Celie," Manon snaps, "if you want to give him the slightest chance to live, go now and get what I need."

That gets me moving. I run, visions of Papa, Maman, and Jacques flashing through my mind so clearly that I feel I will scream. I tap my foot impatiently as the ship's cook heats the water. I pace as clean cloths are pulled out of the captain's trunks. I pull at my hair as a sailor goes in search of a bottle of rum.

When I get back, Jean-Louis is there, and I see that Manon has taken out one of the knives she uses to shape her wax heads.

I hand her the pail of hot water and the clean cloths. Then she takes the bottle of rum from me.

"Celie. Jean-Louis," she says sharply. "I need you to leave."

Jean-Louis obeys and silently climbs aboveboard.

I want to follow him. Every fiber in my being is telling me to run, not to stay here and be forced to see what violence can bring about. But I look at Algernon, see his pale face, his forehead beaded with sweat—my Algernon. His eyes are closed, and he is panting with pain.

And I know, then, that I cannot turn from everything unpleasant in life. To be an adult means troubles have to be faced. Like Manon, I must learn to be strong, to deal with this and any other difficulties that lie ahead. I must be done with running.

I take a deep breath.

"*Non*," I say, and I am proud to hear the resoluteness of my voice. "I'll stay. What do you need me to do?"

Manon looks at me in surprise, and I make myself look steadily back at her without blinking. A spark of admiration comes into her eyes. She nods.

"Take his hand," she says. "This is going to hurt."

There is nothing she could ask of me that I would rather do.

Algernon's skin is hot. He opens his eyes, sees me, and forces a smile to his lips.

Manon pours the alcohol into the wound. Algernon screams, and the grip of his hand in mine grows tight as a noose. Then it suddenly releases, and I see that he has lost consciousness.

I go to shake him back to life, but Manon stays my hand.

"It's better this way," she assures me. "Come. We must get the bullet out."

For the next hour I work beside Manon, helping to hold back the skin as she probes the wound. I am grateful Algernon is not aware of what we are doing. I cannot imagine how much pain he would be in.

When at last I see her draw the bullet out and hear it drop onto the wooden floor beneath our feet, I gasp, as if I have been holding my breath for days.

Manon turns to look at me before she goes about sewing up and dressing the gash. "Do not rest easy just yet, Celie. There is still the risk of infection."

☙

I stand on the deck, and a gust of sea air washes over me. Storm clouds are gathering on the horizon. The crew has told us that we are headed for a squall.

Already the waves are beginning to wash over the bow of the boat, and the ship is heaving from side to side.

There is an ache in my belly as I look back toward the shores of France, though I can no longer see them. I realize that I will probably never again walk the farmlands of my youth, nor the cobblestone streets of Paris. The memories of those days with my family and with Algernon dance before me in all their glory, and all their violence, and all their loss.

The revenge I wished for was not so sweet. Others' lust for power waylaid its charm.

And so I lay down that burden, that sense that some price must be exacted for all my loss. Let others pick up and carry on with the cause. It has lost its appeal for me. Maman and Papa and Jacques have been gone for two years now. I can do no more for them by staying in a country so divided.

Perhaps France will stabilize and rise again as a great nation. Perhaps it will continue on its bloody path and destroy any hope for redemption. I wish with all my heart to see peace in my country, but others will decide that fate—not me, not Algernon.

As for my partner in crime . . . .

I feel a hand upon my arm and turn to look up into the eyes that once rescued me from death. He is pale, but he will live.

"You shouldn't be out here," I reprimand him. "You could fall and rip open your stitches."

He rolls his eyes. "Since when have I avoided danger, Celie?"

He turns me back around and wraps his arms about my waist. He rests his chin upon my shoulder, and together we gaze across the churning water, our future uncertain.

There is a crack of thunder behind us. A wave spills across the bow of the boat.

"We may drown," I say to him.

He laughs softly. "Or we may live. One never knows."

"Where is Jean-Louis?" I ask.

"Below," he says. "I think he is feeling a bit seasick already."

"And Manon?" I ask.

"Watching him carefully. And drawing up plans for a tour around England, promising to build a museum in the city of London that will be grander than the one in the Boulevard du Temple."

I think of our work, safely stowed before our escape to the boat that has smuggled us from France's shores. Surely, the English are no different from the French in that they will be eager to see the wax heads of the late and newly executed king and queen of France. So perhaps, in some small measure, I have had my revenge. The wealthy dead will pay my living now. And I am alive, as is Algernon.

I turn back toward him, my boy rascal, and tilt my head up to his.

He bends his head toward mine and kisses me soundly as the rain begins, one hand firmly on my waist, the fingers of his other hand trailing along my spine in a light pitter-patter that makes my heart thump out a tune of pleasure.

The boat lurches hard to one side. A chill runs up my spine as the wind makes the boards creak, and the sailors shout to one another in panic.

"I have heard a rumor," Algernon whispers in my ear, his voice low and husky from pain and lack of sleep. "They say there is a man coming to England very soon, a man of great wealth."

He pauses. "French wealth."

I realize what he is saying and pull away from him, just as lightening streaks the sky. I am no longer even aware of the rain falling down on us.

I know I am meant to forget. I know I am meant to move on. But if it is truly him, if we live through this storm and land safely in England, how can I ignore the information Algernon has just given me?

I had heard stories, but with everything that has happened, I had all but forgotten them. I try to recall what I had heard: that he had escaped his would-be captors through his brother's insistence that he flee, that he had stolen away to Austria and taken with him thousands of gold coins of the realm, that he was safe and unharmed and living the high life.

Algernon grins wickedly at the flush he must see coming to my cheeks. "Ah, as I suspected. We are not finished with our fun just yet, Celie, are we?"

Rain is coming down hard now. The boat rises up and falls into deeper and deeper troughs. We should be going down below, but neither of us moves.

"I'm done with revenge and revolution, Algernon," I say to him.

"As am I," Algernon says, his voice no longer light but taut with resolve. "Still, it would be a shame to let an opportunity such as this slide by. For I have heard this man is to be staying at a certain house in London. I have made inquiries, and have a friend there who would not be unhappy to have a new maid on his staff, a maid with access to the room of the great and noble—"

"Comte d'Artois," I finish for him. I laugh loudly as flashes of lightening strike the sea with deafening noise.

Algernon's eyes dance with merriment. Rain soaks his hair and runs down his face. "We have not become so incredibly dull that we are giving up on a little fun at the great Comte's expense, have we?"

The storm roars above us. The sailors call for us to go below, to stay safe.

My boy knows me well. Danger has always been what we crave.

Excitement is setting me on fire. I can feel it deep in my gut, can see it in his lips, which twitch with mirth. He pulls me roughly to him, and I go willingly. He buries his fingers in my hair, and brushes his lips upon my neck.

Rain pours down by the bucketful, soaking us, daring us. And I am dizzy with him and the danger of the storm, and with the thrill of perhaps again matching wits with the Comte d'Artois.

And so it seems, as I give in to Algernon's touch and the possibility that this storm may pull us down to watery graves, that if we live, we will plot yet again. For though the revolutionary boy and the girl seeking revenge have died, there is still a bit of the rebel and the thief left in us both.

Author's Note

Marie (Manon) Grosholtz Tussaud led a fascinating life. Her father died before Manon was born in Switzerland in 1761, and her mother went to work as a housekeeper for Dr. Philippe Curtius.

Dr. Curtius was known for his waxmaking skills, often sculpting anatomical parts so that young medical apprentices could practice surgical procedures. (Operating on cadavers was illegal at that time.) In 1763, a French count saw Dr. Curtius's work and commissioned him to come to Paris. Four years later, Dr. Curtius sent for Manon and her mother. Manon was six years old.

On arriving in France, Dr. Curtius's wax figures caught the attention of the king, and commissions for wax likenesses began pouring in. To fill the high demand for his work, Dr. Curtius began teaching Manon the art of waxmaking, eventually letting her mold a likeness of the great writer, Voltaire.

When the king's sister, Élisabeth, expressed interest in learning the process, it was Manon, at the age of twenty, who was sent to be her tutor. (Dr. Curtius was busy creating and opening his new museum, La Caverne des Grands Voleurs.) Manon worked for Madame Élisabeth for ten years, living at Versailles for long periods of time. The king was indeed a master locksmith, a passion of his that he spent many hours perfecting.

Life continued in this vein right up until the Revolution, which brought great change to everyone's life.

It is true that Manon was forced by the National Assembly to make wax models from the executed heads of the royal family. After years of working in the palace, and in particular with Madame Élisabeth, one can only imagine her horror at having to do this. When Madame Élisabeth was beheaded, Manon refused to mold her friend.

Manon was arrested as a Royalist and spent several weeks in jail. In the book, I had Celie arrange her release, although in truth it was Dr. Curtius who was able to obtain her freedom. While in prison, Manon met a woman named Joséphine de Beauharnais, who later became the wife of Napoleon. In time, Manon would mold him as well.

France was in constant turmoil during and following the Revolution. Because of the length of time over which many of the events took place, I have compressed the timeline of the Revolution to make for easier reading.

As entertainment dollars began to dry up, Manon decided to sail to England and take her wax replicas on tour, which she did for many years. On one tour to Ireland, Manon's ship sank, but she managed to make it to shore, even though she lost most of her wax figures and many of the passengers drowned. Eventually Manon settled in London, opening a permanent museum that today has branches all over the world. By then she had married a man named François Tussaud, and taken on the now famous name of Madame Tussaud. (I had her named Tussaud from the beginning in order for readers, familiar with her museums, to recognize who she was). She and François had two sons.

As Celie discovered, revolution is not an easy path. Although Madame Élisabeth was indeed the last royal beheaded, the young prince and heir to the throne died in prison, and the young princess was eventually released and exiled to Austria. It was years before France knew peace again.

Should you have the chance to visit London in the future, be sure to stop by Madame Tussaud's wax museum. The figures of the late king and queen of France are on display even today, their faces molded from their severed heads and then recreated in wax—just for *your* viewing pleasure!

Further Reading and Resources Used

Berridge, Kate. *Madame Tussaud: A Life in Wax.* New York: William Morrow, 2006.

Ransom, Teresa. *Madame Tussaud: A Life and a Time.* Gloucestershire: Sutton Publishing, 2003.

Thorne, Tony. *Who Was… Madame Tussaud: Waxwork Queen of the French Revolution.* London: Short Books, 2003.